Tales from the Silver State

Tales from the Silver State

Tales from the Silver State

Short Fiction from Nevada's Freshest Voices

Jessica Cline • Deborah Coonts
Sheryl Greenblatt • Lindsay Wright
Holly McKinnis • Richard J. Warren
Eric James Miller • John Hill

Edited by Richard J. Warren

Muddy Pig Press • Las Vegas, Nevada

Tales from the Silver State

Photo Credit: trekandshoot

ISBN-13:978-0615941714

ISBN-10: 0615941710

Printed in the United States of America

www.muddypigpress.com

Muddy Pig Press • Las Vegas, Nevada

Dedicated to the Memory
of Jay MacLarty

When you have a dream you have to grab it and never let go.
– Carol Burnett

Contents

Editor's Note

When people think of Las Vegas the image that comes to mind is often one of neon lights, casinos, showgirls and fortunes won or lost. Those who live here know the city is so much more than that. The desert locale of this gambler's Mecca is also home to a thriving writer's community. Within that community lies a phenomenon known as the Las Vegas Writers Group. It was the vision of Jay MacLarty, author of a series of thrillers published by Simon & Shuster. Jay envisioned a place where writers could come together to learn from one another and support each other as they practiced their craft.

Many writers have passed through this group on their way to finding success as authors. With the aid of the group and its members they honed their craft and expanded their knowledge of the business of writing. Several of them have been invited to celebrate Jay's legacy by sharing the stories you will find in these pages.

Assembling an anthology would not be possible without the help and support of others. Acknowledgement and thanks to the contributing authors: Jessica Cline, Deborah Coonts, Sheryl Greenblatt, John Hill, Holly McKinnis, Eric James Miller, Richard J. Warren, and Lindsay Wright. The foreword was written by Vic Cravello, one of the founders of

1

The Las Vegas Writers Group and close friend of Jay. Vic also provided a tremendous amount of input for this project.

Special thanks go to Dr. Maile Chapman, professor in the Creative Writing Program at the University of Nevada Las Vegas and the editor of Witness Magazine. Her invaluable assistance with this project is greatly appreciated.

Thanks to the "piglets" on staff at the Muddy Pig Press for making this anthology possible.

Foreword

By Vic Cravello

When I retired from the corporate world my dear wife suggested I write a book. After all, I had nothing else to do. How hard could it be anyway? Obviously we were clueless, like 90% of the wannabe's who drop out in the first year and forever wonder why nobody gave a rap about "their memoirs."

Seeing no progress for a few weeks, my wife again asked, "are you still on page one?" I am I confessed, but I lied. I hadn't even cracked the cover of the daunting book on writing she had gotten for me. "Well then why don't you check this out," handing me a brochure for the *Las Vegas Book Festival* that would change everything. I gave it a feeble squint, too far away. "I'll go with you," she offered. We went, thank goodness!

At the book festival one of the speakers was Jay MacLarty, an unassuming low-key guy with a full blonde beard. He quietly told his story about getting two novels published with two more in the works. He was also working on his *pièce de rèsistance* – a thousand-page mega story about a woman searching for her place in the world and a shot at breaking through the glass ceiling of corporate America. It turned out he was not only a great speaker, but a prolific writer. Wow, I thought! I need to talk to this guy, but everyone in the room wanted to talk to him too. I got my chance after waiting in line a bit. Jay and I hit it off immediately.

Now I should stress that Jay appeared unassuming and low key. Beneath that calm exterior was a burning intensity. For example, Jay worked out every day after a morning of writing. He proudly announced one year that he had worked out 365 days without missing once. This passion ran through every aspect of his life.

Jay invited me to join the fledgling Las Vegas Writers Group, of which he was a member along with ten others, give or take, meeting wherever they could find a place, often some unsavory bar or backroom. After a few months Jay said, "We've just scratched the surface and I know we can do better, there should be a hundred people here at least. I needed help when I first started out and these people do too. I want this group to give them that help and be a real resource to the writing community. We can do this, we have to do this. It's my way of giving back and repaying people for the help I had – I *want* to do this. . . before I die." He was looking directly at me, his piercing blue eyes filled with that intensity. "I need your help, Vic, to make it happen." I was skeptical, but there was no denying him!

Jay had been a corporate guy, like me, and he valued people with organizational and business skills like himself. But for the writers group he envisioned personally working with

4

writers behind the scenes rather than running the show. He loved nothing better than to hold court after the regular meetings and talk shop. That's how I became the Organizer and we began to build, one aspiring writer at a time. His thought was to involve the people who really want to help and give the members real value for their $5 admission. We reinvest that meeting fee to cover expenses, host an annual holiday party and produce this anthology. The model worked far beyond our expectations; we outgrew venue after venue.

Membership has soared to more than 350 writers with monthly meeting attendance averaging 70 members. Along the way we also recruited some great people like John Hill, an Emmy Award-winning screenwriter who has been a tremendous asset to the group, Lindsay Wright, the current Program Director who has recruited a number of impressive speakers, and Sheryl Greenblatt, the Critique Group Organizer and board member of the *Writers of Southern Nevada*. All three have been winners of the *Jay MacLarty Founder's Award* recognizing their contributions to the local literary community. Lastly, we passed the Organizer's baton from me to Richard Warren in order to broaden our experience base and provide the leadership needed to navigate the changing world of writing. Richard was a great choice due to his extremely active involvement in the local literary scene. He has taken Jay's concept to an even higher level. Unfortunately we lost Jay to brain cancer in the process, but his dream was fulfilled. He would also have been very pleased that the premise of his mega-book came to fruition recently when General Motors actually promoted a woman to CEO, the first one ever in a car company. No surprise there, Jay was always a visionary.

We salute Jay and thank him for his leadership; the Las Vegas Writers Group would not have happened without him. It is his Legacy.

Cody Banktree's Loader

by John Hill

It was sunset before I got back to our small Nevada ranch that cold fall evening in 1936. The sky was a color Dad called "blood on a rusty spur." There was no work in Carson City that day. A Depression causes depression, I thought to myself. I parked the old Ford pickup, and looked around for my son, Charlie, wondering if he was in Dad's small cabin in back, bothering my father, instead of feeding the few chickens we had left. Dad was sixty-six, and a genuine cowboy old-timer. He had stories about the Old West, he knew it, he was there. Some stories were really funny. But this was the day my son, Charlie, would lose his innocence. I knew it the moment I walked up to the door of Dad's cabin in back and heard part of the story I had told him never to tell Charlie.

"...anyway, Charlie boy, my Pappy had died a year before, so I had to work, do a man's work too, sweeping out the saloon, emptyin' spittoons, anything," my father was saying to my son as I stepped inside. The cabin was small, cozy, the pot-bellied stove glowing red. Dad motioned for me to sit on the bed. The place smelled of pipe tobacco and worn-out glory.

7

"Dad," I said. "Not the Cody Banktree story. I asked you not to –"

Charlie's eyes lit up as he looked at me. "Yeah, Dad! Cody Banktree! Grampa says he was tall as a tree and meaner'n an acre of snakes!"

My father laughed. I sighed, staring at my father, who shrugged at me, then sipped some bourbon. He had long, gray-white Buffalo Bill hair now, and wore his usual cheap red plaid shirt, old jeans and a good pair of boots.

"Boy's gonna hear this story sometime, son," Dad said to me quietly. I motioned for him to step outside with me and told Charlie to just wait here. Once we were outside, in the cold, his cabin door closed, the sunset a red blaze in one small part of a dark blue sky, I said, "He never has to hear that story, Dad. I don't want him to."

"I already started it," Dad said. "He's my grandson! That story says a lot about the old West, and I'm not going to live forever. What if I die before I tell people, people close to me, things that I did in my life?"

"Lot of things you did," I said, "might be better no one ever knows, right?"

He laughed, then it turned into a deep cough.

"I'm cold out here," he said, "let's get back to the stove."

"You're just wanting to brag. Pick a different story –"

"So what if I am? At my age, what else I got? Of course I want Charlie to look up to me. I was part of history!"

8

"Tell him about the one-legged Shawnee warrior –"

"You ever realize how short a time the Wild West really was? We sure didn't know it at the time. From after the Civil War to about 1905? Forty years. Then, one day, there's police in towns instead of sheriffs, cars instead of horses, hell, airplanes, telephones, the West as we know it, long gone. But these cowboy books, movies, toys and legends, they make it look like it lasted a thousand years –"

"Not the Cody Banktree story, Dad," I said, starting to go inside. "I'm serious."

He came right back at me with his low, mean tone. "And I'm serious about whether I'll keep givin' you cash each month if you get between me and Charlie," he said. "Unless you finally got yourself a job. No?" Dad smiled his cold gunfighter smile, went on inside his cabin. I sighed, and followed. Would Dad tell a different story? Should I risk the money he gave me to stop him? I really didn't want Charlie hearing that story. I went in.

Charlie's face lit up. "Grampa, please tell me the Cody Banktree story!"

Dad sat back down in his old rocking chair by the pot bellied stove, motioned for me to sit on the bed, and slowly lit his big old curved pipe. I sat and waited. He had a thousand stories, a lot of them probably true. He didn't have to tell this one story and he knew it and I knew it.

"It was near Carson City, in 1878," my father began, looking at Charlie. "Cody Banktree was the fastest, meanest

9

gunfighter there was in all of Nevada. He loved to practice his fast draw in a small ravine, just outside of town. One day, when I was just eight, a little younger than you are now, Charlie," Dad said, puffing on his pipe, "I watched Cody Banktree practice drawing and shooting his Navy Colt revolver. Lightning fast! Then I asked him if I could load it for him. He said, 'Sure, Half-Pint! Here's how to do it!' And he showed me and let me load his gun for him. Then he tried a really tough shot, some far rock, hit it and laughed. He said I brought him luck! Well, from that day forward, I was Cody Banktree's loader!"

Charlie's eyes were glowing. He loved this story already. Usually, his favorite stories involved Dad's run-in's with the Kiowa. Dad then told Charlie about the hard talk Cody Banktree had with the Bar 9 boys at the saloon one day. "Some pushin' and shovin' and tough talk," Dad said. "One thing led to another, and it was time for one of 'em to step out into the street, against Cody Banktree. I asked Mr. Banktree if I could be his loader, for luck. He laughs and said 'Sure, Half-Pint!' He handed me his gun and bullets while he had another drink."

Charlie couldn't stand it while Dad slowly paused to play with his pipe, then finally get it lit, then finally returned to his narrative. I couldn't stand it because I knew how much Charlie looked up to his grandfather. How do I stop this?

"It was a windy day, wet and muddy," Dad continued on, his face hidden for a moment by the puffs of curling smoke.

10

The fire crackled. "Well, that young cowpoke from the Bar 9, he walked down about fifty feet, and he turned and gulped, trying to get ready. That cowpoke was scared. Cody Banktree strolled out, stood in the street, then he did the damndest thing – he stopped to slowly roll a cigarette and light it! He put it between his lips, then looks at the cowpoke, and loudly allowed as how the cowpoke's mother ate refried buffalo shit for dinner. Well, shots were fired, horses reared up, gun smoke – then Cody Banktree, with this surprised look on his face, falls face forward into the mud, two blood-red holes in his chest. Died right there, cigarette still in his mouth."

Dad paused, puffed on his pipe, looked at Charlie, grinned and winked, but Charlie could only stare. And wait. Another puff, the smoke angling up like a gray air dancer, then Dad continued.

"Only one man, the saloon owner who took me in when my Pappy died, later noticed that Cody Banktree's gun had never been fired, or loaded. He never told on me. You see, the saloon owner knew that Cody Banktree had shot and killed my Pappy a year before. Took me a year, but I made sure Cody Banktree wouldn't ever shoot anyone else's Pappy. I was eight, a year younger than you are now, Charlie."

Charlie's grin sort of froze on his face as the full realization hit him. Charlie would never look at his grandfather quite the same way. I'd first heard that story when I was thirteen. It had changed things a little between me and my father forever, only he never knew it. Dad was proud of that

11

story. He liked to say he got himself a notch on his gun before he ever had a gun. I gave my father a sad look, but he just grinned, pleased, then sucked on a pint of Jim Beam. Then he coughed a deep cough. He was my father and wouldn't live forever. I motioned for Charlie to leave my Dad's little cabin, and I followed. I knew we'd talk later.

"Go feed the chickens, son," I said, as I walked to the main house through the dark red evening to see about supper. I turned the collar of my jacket up. Maybe I'd find work in town tomorrow.

The Ghost of John Bartlett

By Eric James Miller

"Lost mister?"

The gruff voice shook John out of his reverie. He hadn't noticed the man crossing the street towards him until the large, sweaty beast was almost upon him.

The smell of cheap liquor on the man's breath so early in the day irritated John and reminded him of the hundreds of rogues he had worked alongside on the docks back in St. Louis. Still, such men could be useful sometimes. For one, they almost always knew the very best shortcuts around town.

"Not lost," John replied, "just new around these parts. Would you be so kind and direct me towards Fremont Street please?"

"New around here, uh?" The man's gaze dropped to John's sturdy new leather and fabric traveling case sitting on the rough-hewed wooden planks that served as a sidewalk in front of the rail station.

"Say, that's a nice bag you got there. Mind if I see what's in it?"

John Bartlett did mind. But he also realized he was being challenged not five minutes after arriving in a town

13

where men still wore dusty cowboy hats and chewed their words slowly.

His whole life he had been an avid reader of stories about cowboys, Indians, and life in the west. Now he was finally standing in one of those wild west towns himself. The fact amused him. Destiny clearly had an unpredictable sense of humor. Though the century had just changed to a modern one, he appreciated being initiated to town in one of the old ways.

He had a choice. He could react politely, as he had been taught. Or he could react directly, as he had learned.

He smiled at the irony of the modern age.

Only three nights from Salt Lake City. Hell, just two more and I could have gone all the way to California!

Staring at the near sleepless faces of his fellow passengers for all those hours on the belching iron horse had taken a surprising toll on them all. He hadn't brought enough water with him for the journey. No one had. Plus, the meal service provided by the railroad company was thin at best and came with just two sloppy ladles of half-dank water. The lack of decent food and fresh water, combined with the constant clanging, rattling and churning that was part of speeding into the horizon by rail made the trip exhausting.

Ironically, the thick-neck bully now testing his resolve was actually a welcomed, albeit rather rude, change that merely confirmed arrival at his destination.

14

So this is Las Vegas, Nevada. Mercy me, it is truly splendid!

The assortment of brightly painted buildings, together with the colorful, bustling crowd, light breeze in his hair and the soaring blue sky not only outweighed the rigors of John Bartlett's journey, it even outweighed the withering furnace of heat baking both down from the sky and up from the ground.

The heat. He had been warned about it. Again and again in fact.

The heat was, indeed, very, very impressive.

For someone who had grown up on the outskirts of a small prairie town called Spirit Lake, Iowa it was an unprecedented experience. It was even different from the many suffocating summers he spent working the docks in St. Louis to finance his bold new start on the modern day western frontier.

Sweating without perspiration. What next? 1907 had already proven itself to be the best year John Bartlett could remember. Plus, it was only early June. There were almost seven months of promise still left in it. Clearly, accepting an offer from a distant uncle to help run a trade store along the Clark Road had been the best decision he had made in a long time.

It seemed like only the first step towards finding his fortune in the new twentieth century.

"I said, do you mind if I look through your bag?" the

gruff, foul-smelling lout repeated as he bent down and picked up John's bag.

"Hey! Now wait just a minute. That's mine." John shot his left arm out and clinched a corner of the fabric bag in his fist.

The brute batted John's arm away and smiled. His several missing teeth served as warning not to argue any further. He turned and began clodding his way down the street as he fumbled with the latch on John's bag.

John sucked in a big breath of air and looked around the vibrant, bustling town of corrugated tin shacks, lean-to's and fine, mill lumber built buildings. It certainly felt more alive than anywhere in St. Louis on a Saturday night. John took his pocket watch from his pocket and checked the time. It was only just before noon on a Tuesday!

Lively music spilled out onto the street from every direction. People of all colors and stripes scurried about despite the almost knee-buckling heat. Some were obviously richer than others. Some looked in need of a decent meal. But most looked like they were working, either very busy with their own concerns or those of their employers. Even real live Apache Indians seemed to have business to attend to in and out of the myriad of shops clustered around the train station.

Job notices for miners, laborers, account managers and just about every other position John could imagine were posted everywhere.

He looked up and squinted into the sky. But not

because he was searching for help from the heavens. With a guaranteed job already and so much opportunity right at his feet, John knew he could replace most of what was in his luggage within a month.

But it was the principal of being robbed his first day in town — just scant minutes after getting off the train to start his new life — that prevented him from walking away.

"Everything I own is in that bag," John explained as he sprang after the man and turned him sternly by his filthy shoulder.

The man grunted and shoved his meaty paw against John's chest. He grinned. "Yes, well and now it's mine. Do yourself a favor and don't make me mad."

The man reached under his filthy, nearly button-less, long ago white shirt. He brandished a long, ragged edged piece of sharpened scrap metal. "This here bag is mine now. Take that fine suit you're wearing and get back on your little choo-choo. Before I decide that there suit is mine too."

John sighed. "I abhor violence."

"What? Did you just call me what I think you called me, mister?"

"I didn't call you anything, sir. But, if I were to choose words with which to slander you, 'stupid', 'oaf' and, well, 'quite ugly and foul smelling' are the first to pop to mind."

The man turned beet red and dropped John's bag on the wooden sidewalk. "Okay, mister. I don't know where you're from, but you're going back there with your toes pointed up to

17

the sky."

John stepped off the makeshift sidewalk and into the dusty street. The bear sized ruffian who had so rudely welcomed him to town happily followed.

"Would any of you happen to know where the local deputy or town sheriff is by chance?" John asked the crowd swelling on both sides of the street to watch the imminent clash between yet another new-comer and one of their own.

The wagon, horse and buggy, and even Stanley Steamer traffic collectively held its breath and paused to watch.

A low murmur rose from the crowd. But John heard no discernible response. Before anyone could answer him directly, if any of them even intended to, the man lunged at John with the ugly make-shift blade.

It didn't take a college education to anticipate such a clumsy direct attack. But John wanted the certificate in his bag stating that he had one just in case he needed it sometime down the road.

He took half a step to the side to dodge the assault, twisted the man's wrist and used his opponent's momentum to propel him several feet down the street.

Furious at falling flat on his ass in a cloud of dust in front of so many people, the embarrassed thug stood up, dusted himself off and charged back towards John.

Since the man was several inches taller than John, wielding the blade like a hammer over his head must have

18

seemed like a clear, perhaps even overwhelming advantage both to him and those watching. Several women in the crowd gasped and cried out pointless warnings. But John had encountered large opponents who over relied on their size advantage in a fight before. He simply had to stand his ground and wait for the man to get close enough to stab the knife downwards before retaliating.

Time slowed down. Milliseconds seemed reluctant to break a sweat in the heat. Befriending several wise old Chinese men on those docks back in St. Louis, when no one else would, had proven beneficial time and time again. Always an avid learner, apprenticing with them on some ancient fighting wisdom they called crane style kung fu was something John would always honor and never, ever forget.

It had also proven itself to be a great way to add to his bank account when there wasn't anything better to do on a Saturday night than step into a boxing ring against a burly, over-confident opponent.

John studied his opponent's approach. The art of kung fu honed not only physical acumen, but also mental acumen. Despite the jests and jeers from his Irish friends and brothers he had taken it quite seriously for several years. The wise old Chinese men that taught it to him had even given him a ceremonial cloth belt after he told them he would be leaving the docks to pursue his dreams out west.

The thin black memento was something else in his luggage bag that he had no intention of losing.

19

The angry bull of a man charged on towards him puffing and shouting with fury. When the expected hammer blow started to descend, John planted his right foot behind him, crouched and raised one arm above his head as he drove the palm of his right hand squarely into the middle of the man's chest.

Stopped in his tracks with every ounce of air forced from his lungs, the man clutched his chest and fell to his knees. The homemade knife slipped from his fingers as he stared up at John in disbelief.

John stared down at his gasping adversary and shook his head in disgust. Then the sound of applause distracted him. He glanced across the street. Sure enough, several finely dressed ladies and dapper gentlemen were clapping in approval as they cautiously approached.

"Well, done, my lad!" one of them boasted. "That rogue hasn't met his match on these streets in far too long."

The man John had just brought to his knees glared at the crowd. He picked up the saw-tooth blade lying on the ground next to him and pointed it at John.

John calmly stepped forward. As the man swiped the air in front of him, John grabbed the man's wrist, twisted it straight up in the air and rested the palm of his left hand against the man's elbow joint. "If you drop that broken scythe in your hand right now, I'll be less likely to break your arm," John whispered.

The lout obeyed immediately. "I'm sorry," he pleaded.

20

"I'm just hungry. I lost all my money in a rigged card game. I'm new here, too. Just like you. Let's be pals, okay? We can be pals can't we? You and me. I'll show you around. I know everybody worth knowing in this crummy town. I'll introduce you as a fine and proper gentleman and we'll share the best brandy. How's that sound?"

John let go of the man's wrist. "Gambling is the devil's work. If you're so hungry, use some of the money you've been spending on cheap whiskey to buy yourself some food."

"I will. I will, buddy. I promise."

As the big man stood up, the people crossing the street hesitated and were caught between several wagons and carriages continuing on with their business in opposite directions.

John stepped back up on the sidewalk to retrieve his bag.

"Look out!" a woman screamed.

John glanced towards the woman's sweet as a bird voice. A tall, slender young beauty with long wavy jet black hair cascading over her bold, off the shoulder corset dress held one delicate hand to her mouth as she pointed with the other behind him. Her creamy porcelain skin and fluttering dark eyes momentarily mesmerized him as he let go of his bag, ducked and stepped to the side. Only then did he glance over his shoulder to assess the situation.

Sure enough his newest friend was proving to be no friend at all. He had picked up the sharpened piece of metal

21

and was charging towards John with renewed vigor.

John jumped down off the sidewalk to street level. He waited an extra second, then sprang straight up in the air.

The flat, hard, square tip of his right boot delivered the full force of a perfectly executed flying front kick directly under the man's chin.

The oaf was cross-eyed and unconscious before his back hit the ground.

The stunning woman who had dared to warn John in time to save him from being stabbed stepped over to the man sprawled on the ground. She spat in his face and dug the heel of her boot into his right hand. "Pig!"

She turned to John and smiled a smile so disarming John almost collapsed to the ground as well. "You sir," she purred as she stalked over to her prey like a cat and wrapped her arm in his, "are the bravest man I've met in a month of Sundays. What, pray tell is your name and where are you staying?"

John bent down and picked up his luggage, careful not to disrupt her hold on his arm. "My name is John Bartlett, ma'am. My uncle runs a place called the Dusty Rail over on Fremont Street. I just got off the train and was heading over there. He wrote me in St. Louis and said he had a job for me if I was willing to come out West."

"Well, my, my. Isn't that a coincidence?" the young woman replied as she glared at the other pretty young women gathered around. "I was just heading over to the Dusty Rail myself. Seems I'm in desperate need of some beauty powder and maybe a glass or two of fine French champagne. Would you care to accompany me?"

"Well, since I don't exactly know the way myself, I'd be much obliged," John replied. He noticed the crowd parted for them like a plough blade cutting through chaff after harvest. He also noticed more than a few looks of regret in the eyes of the young women who had been less quick to greet him. "And what may I ask is your name?" he added.

He had seen plenty of buxom women in bold corset dresses like hers in front of the taverns and motels that rented rooms by the hour along the docks of St. Louis. Their lace gloves and low-cut, expensive velvet dresses cinched tight at the waist usually told their whole story. But this gal seemed a little different. Not just because none were quite so exotic and beautiful as the one holding his arm right at that moment. None had ever smelled so nice as her, at least as far as he knew, and none had ever, ever saved his life before.

"Rose. Rose Anne Paulson, if you really must know," she answered with a demure smile. "That's my real name. Most people 'round these parts know me as Miss Amy Lynn. But I'd rather you call me Rose. If that's alright with you, of course."

"Pleased to meet you, Miss Paulson. Do you mind if I ask where you're from? You're just about the prettiest thing I've ever seen in my whole life. And I must say, that purple dress of yours is, I do believe, my new favorite color."

"Oh, why thank you, Mr. Bartlett. My mother is from a place called Sweden. It's somewhere over in Europe on the other side of the Atlantic Ocean. Apparently everyone in the whole country has blonde hair and blue eyes. Can you believe that? My father, he was an officer in the Spanish army over here teaching the Mexican army how to do surveying so as to make better maps. Unfortunately, he had to go back to Spain. He's trying to find a way to quit the army and come back to America. But so far, all my mother gets is the occasional letter. That's how I've come to be an entrepreneur of sorts. If you need any maps made, or anything else, you come see me first, okay?"

John turned his head to hide his smile. Normally, he'd be embarrassed to be seen walking down the street arm in arm with a woman like Miss Amy Lynn, no matter how pretty she was.

But walking down the street with Miss Rose Anne Paulson was another matter entirely. It felt like his destiny. "I can't see any reason why a man in his right mind would do anything sideways to that generous offer."

"Mmm, so you're saying you're a man in your right mind. What a refreshing change from most of the John's I meet around here."

John abruptly stopped walking and for a moment considered ending his engagement with the second person he had met in Las Vegas in order to hope for better luck with the third.

She patted his arm. "Now don't be twisting anything I just said around in that handsome head of yours. I didn't mean anything crude by that silly remark. After what you did back there to that mean old bastard Jerzy Kaczynski, you are my for all-time and evermore hero."

John smiled and this time let her see that he was very pleased to have made her acquaintance.

"Any chance there's a place around here where a fellow can get a nice big cool glass of water, or better yet, a bath?" he asked as he let her steer him down Main Street. "The water they had on the train must have been run through the steam engines first because not only was it piping hot, it tasted down right awful."

Rose grinned and leaned into him, tightening her grip on his arm. "Well, yes sir. Las Vegas has the best water this side of the Rocky Mountains. Do you know what Las Vegas means in Spanish, my dashing young hero from St. Louis?"

John stole a glance down the front of her dress. He didn't regret it, but he instantly chided himself for it. He thought of the sturdy, tireless Mormon women on the train that had made the trip west with him and forced himself to act like a gentleman, despite the immediate proximity of his left arm to her ample womanly charms.

After we are married, if we are to be married, there will be plenty of time for that sort of familiarity in the future.

"No, ma'am. What does it mean?" he asked.

"It means 'The Meadows' and it's because of all the

water hiding under this here insanely hot, insanely dry Mojave desert. It's why the steam trains stop here on their way to California. It's the only water for near about two hundred miles ... unless you count that old muddy Colorado River way over yonder."

She waved a dainty, lace gloved hand towards the eastern horizon and John stole a glance in that direction to see if he could see any sign of it. Though there wasn't a tree more than fifteen feet tall clear to the shimmering white horizon, he had to take her word that an infamous deep river flowed somewhere over in that direction.

John looked behind him and saw that he and his new friend were being followed by about a dozen other smiling, whispering, finely dressed ladies and dapper-dans.

John smiled. "Is that so? Well then isn't this just the perfect place to be then?"

"It surely is," she cooed. "It surely, surely is."

Unfortunately, despite a promising start John's time in Las Vegas turned out mighty short. His uncle put him behind the bar of the Dusty Rail and taught him how to order new inventory for the always busy, often under-stocked trade store. With Rose's help, John learned who to trust and who not to in the burgeoning little rail town that connected the booming, strike-it-rich mining towns like Bullfrog to the north and the verdant California farmlands to the west.

There was even talk about making John a candidate

for office since the town had only been independent from the railroad for two years and there were few educated men about who weren't mere pawns of the railroad interests.

Like everything he committed to, he threw himself into work and took a room above the bar so as to better learn the rhythms of life in his new home. It was a twenty-four hour town to be sure. Because of the heat, there were two economies, one during the day and one at night.

The one at night was definitely the much more interesting, and lucrative, of the two.

Walks started getting longer and longer with Miss Rose Anne Paulson, who worked less and less for a sharp, but kind-hearted businesswoman named Miss Arthur Johnson. By the end of summer he had found some land with its own well to homestead just outside the south end of town. While keeping up with the demands of his new job, he somehow found the hours to start building a house for him and his future wife.

Unfortunately word got around about his homestead and it was there, one evening just after sunset, he found himself cornered by Jerzy and a couple of his equally loutish buddies.

A fierce, desperate fight took place between the four men. John almost walked away from it after snapping one man's neck and breaking Jerzy's right leg at the knee. With no ally there to warn him though, a broad shovel to the back of his head brought him down and before he could fully regain

27

consciousness to fight off the third man he found himself hurtling towards the bottom of his cherished well.

He swam for hours, yelling for help until his voice gave out. By early the next morning, just as the light of a new day spread across the fickle desert, exhaustion overtook him John Bartlett slipped under the water for the last time.

I can't believe I'm drowning in a desert. I just met the woman of my dreams. This can't be happening ....

The heinous crime went unpunished, though Jerzy Kaczynski walked with a severe limp for the rest of his short, miserable life. The ore train that cut him in half didn't even slow down when it hit him.

In contrast, John's sudden disappearance became an enduring mystery. Hope for his miraculous return was kept alive not only by Rose and his uncle, but also several close new friends and an elderly pastor and his family who finished building the simple five room house John had started. The property was run in John Bartlett's name as a shelter for runaway youth and other downtrodden citizens of early Las Vegas well into the 1920's.

Although his dreams of a long, prosperous life in the wide open spaces of the Mojave were dashed, one part of John's dream did manage to come true. After exhausting every legal option they could wrangle out of their powerful and well-connected benefactors, Miss Arthur and Rose saw that the passing of the property deed went to the gentle pastor and his small family.

Unfortunately, after the pastor and his wife died, their golden-haired teenage daughter joined a carnival act on its way to San Francisco and their only son fell victim to the allure of the bright lights and ever ravenous one-armed bandits blinking inside the electrified downtown casino halls. He died an inglorious, untimely and indebted life. But not before fathering one child with a starry-eyed woman passing through on her way to Hollywood, and another by a kind-hearted woman who, before joining a group of missionaries, tried to save him from himself.

The property, unofficially abandoned for years, fell into a public trust and stagnated as the neon infused city of Las Vegas grew around it. A long series of wily drifters used the land to build one shanty town after another. When one burned down, a new one grew in its place almost overnight.

More than a few men and women laid claim to the trust.

In the early 1970's, multiple conflicting claims were settled in court under one umbrella ownership agreement and the odd assortment of buildings were turned into a small, cheap motel that rented rooms to down on their luck gamblers, dodgy salesmen selling the latest fad and others passing in and out of the ever growing neon city. It's unclear what compelled the founders of that ownership agreement to call it the Bartlett Motel. But the many stories of angry shadows ransacking rooms, moaning cries for help and sounds of violent splashing in very deep, very far away water were well-known. At least to those who had ever spent more than a night on the property

Now, years later, ownership of the property is once again a matter for the courts to decide. Unpaid property taxes date back over twenty years and none of those named in that 1970's ownership agreement have stepped forward to take responsibility or lay claim to the property

It's said the ghost of John Bartlett still walks the grounds at night. Only skeptics and others unfamiliar with the property are willing to argue with the claim. He rises up out from the old collapsed well house in back and makes sure his guests are safe. When they aren't, even though it's another new century and almost everything has changed beyond recognition from what he started back in 1907, John Bartlett still does what he can to make things right.

What he hasn't decided yet is which of the pastor's two heirs deserve to inherit the property.

THE END

Psychic Ear

By Holly McKinnis

"Hello," Jessica called into the darkened psychic shop. Funny, she was never the first one in at the Ear. She pulled aside the curtain to her cubby. Two naked bodies writhed on top of her table. For a split second, she wanted to drop the curtain and excuse herself, but realized they were fucking on top of her reading table getting sex juice all over her hand-dyed silk tablecloth. "Hey! What the hell?"

As if her words had activated a shock collar, the man jumped off the girl. "Jessie," he said, trying to cover himself first with his hands, then her tablecloth.

"Damien?" Her partner wilted under her gaze. "What do you think you're doing?"

"It was her idea." He hooked a thumb toward the girl.

Chantelle, the overly-perky palm-reader, seemed unphased. "Hey Jess, you're in early." She sat up, unembarrassed by her nudity.

"Jessica, my name is Jessica." Anger sent blood singing. "I'm not early. I'm –" a quick glance at her watch, "on time."

Chantelle snorted. "For once." She slid off the table with serpentine elegance.

"Get out," Jessica hissed.

The other woman picked up her clothes and left, pausing to shoot a wink at Damien.

He coughed, a combination of nerves and smoking. "Uh, Jessie, I've been meaning to talk to you." He straightened, and the movement pulled the cloth the rest of the way off the table, sending her cards and candles helter-skelter across the floor.

A card came to rest by her foot, the fool. *Thanks, Universe*, she thought. Too little, too late. "What?" she snapped at Damien, who, thinking to assuage her anger, had bent to pick up her belongings.

"Well, you know, ah . . . things have been a little slow between us. I just thought-"

"You thought you'd speed them up with a little cowboy-style humping on my table?"

"Yeah, I mean, no. Damn it, Jessie, you know what I'm trying to say. Why are you making this difficult?"

"Oh, so this is my fault? Spit it out, you weenie."

"Fine. I'm activating the buy-out clause in your contract. For such a fabulous card-reader, I surprised you didn't see this coming. You're done here."

Fired! He was firing her! From deep inside, she felt her power rising. The wind picked up, throwing itself at the windows. "Done?" she felt anger shoot out of her eyes. She turned her attention to the front window. Across the lot sat Damien's brand-new red Mercedes. A dust devil grew and moved with slow deliberation towards the car, slamming into it just as Damien turned.

"No!" He covered his eyes, but she knew he would never wipe away the sight of the convertible-top peeling off and careening into a dumpster. He froze, then picking up a card, he crumpled it, and threw it at her. The Queen of Pentacles landed next to the Fool. Reversed, of course.

Her breath caught in her throat. She spent hours attuning her cards to spirit forces. Her cards were accurate and true. How dare he? Catching sight of a semi loaded full of produce, she wished. And, as if she had blown out all the candles on her birthday cake, her wish came true. The dust-devil threw a plastic bag at the semi's windshield blinding the driver, who flinched and over-corrected. Jessica smiled, listening to the crunch of the back wheels running over the hood of the Mercedes. "Now I'm done."

"You bitch!" He stood and threw up his hands, calling down the forces of destruction.

She froze, waiting for his power to strike. Seconds passed, and nothing happened. "That's it? That's all you got?" She snickered and started collecting her belongings, throwing them into a tote bag.

He swept out of the room. From outside in the store, she heard him crashing around. He panted and muttered, every other word or so audible. "Bitch," mutter mutter, "she thinks," mumble, grunt, crash, scrape.

When she had loaded everything she owned, she gave a quick scan of her room. Nothing else she wanted. Two years worth of work packed up in two minutes. Time to start over. Only this time she would have control. Maybe start her own shop; get her own stable of psychics. Call it, Aura Knowledge. That sounded good. No, Crystal Aura. Yes, a name that would evoke crystal balls and spirituality. Starting to hum *It's a Long, Long Way To Tipperary*, she slung the strap of her bag over her shoulder, flipped off the light, and stepped into a scene from a horror flick.

Damien's efforts had transformed the shop from a trinket/book store, into a satanic temple complete down to the wood-inlayed pentagram on the floor. He stood in the middle, holding Chantel with a hand over her mouth and struggling to cut her with a ceremonial knife. "You made me do this! This is your fault."

Chantel took advantage of his loss of focus and slammed down on his instep with her bare foot. At the same time, she bit the hand over her mouth. "Help me! He's crazy."

Damien grabbed her by her hair and forced her to the ground, putting a knee in her back. "Hey, that hurt," he said, examining his hand. Noticing the blood welling up, he shrugged and started to draw the runes that would wake his demon.

"Jess, please, help me." Chantelle twisted her head pleading eyes gazing up toward the other witch.

34

"Oh, you kids. So young; so in love." Jessica pulled open the door. "Chantelle?"

They both looked up. "My name is Jessica." The door shut behind her with the sound of tinkling bells, barely audible over a despairing scream.

*****

Tales from the Silver State

Lucky Like That

A Lucky O'Toole Original Short Story

By Deborah Coonts

The gal was clever. She almost fooled me.

Dressed in the normal cocktail waitress attire—a dab of Lycra, five-inch stilettos and a smile—she blended into the normal craziness of a large Vegas Strip casino on a Friday night. I almost missed her. The Flamingo isn't my usual stomping grounds so I didn't have my bullshit meter on high alert. And I was late for an appointment with a man in a dress. Some guy who billed himself as The Great Teddie Divine. My assistant, Miss P, thought he'd make the perfect headliner at the Babylon, Las Vegas's newest and most over-the-top Strip property. I thought she'd lost her mind, especially since the Big Boss, the man we all answered to, had let me know in no uncertain terms he was looking for high-class.

I didn't think a guy in heels and a dress qualified.

Running ragged trying to get the Babylon ready—we were mere weeks away from our opening gala—I'd resisted Miss P's pleas. Frankly, I'd held out longer than I thought possible. With work and all, I couldn't remember the last time

I'd spent any meaningful time staring at the inside of my eyelids, so my defenses were down. Miss P had gotten all quiet and sulky. Okay, <u>she</u> hadn't gotten sulky, <u>I</u> had, even a bit testy, but that hadn't scared her, which I sorta liked. At a stalemate, the only way to move forward was to give in.

And there was this pesky little issue—we needed some show-stopping entertainment for the hordes of guests who would, if prayers were answered, stampede our property on opening day.

So I had caved, but that didn't spur me to hurry now that I was late. I was supposed to meet Ms. Divine between shows—that window was rapidly closing, so I'd have to wait until the late show was over which I doubted would put me in the good graces of the man in a dress... I'd heard he could be a bit of a drama queen. I smiled at the pun. What can I say? I'm easily amused.

My name is Lucky O'Toole and I'm the Head of Customer Relations at the Babylon... in theory, since we've yet to host a customer. Right now my job pretty much consisted of solving problems, which certainly played to my strengths.

If trouble beckons, I heed the call—it's knee-jerk at this point, so I rarely waste energy resisting. And a lifetime of dealing with low-lifes had honed my radar to a fine pitch as if the devil himself was perched on my shoulder whispering in my ear, raising the hairs on the back of my neck—a warning

I'd learned to ignore only at my peril. And peril wasn't on my personal to-do list tonight.

So, ready to hit the push-bar on the theater door, I paused, stopped by that familiar internal warning. Stepping to the side, I turned to give the crowd another once over. From where I stood I could see the poster for the show—one side was in costume, a sequined off-the-shoulder gown, important jewelry around his neck, straight black hair and chandelier earrings flanking a pretty face in full female war-paint—Cher overdone, if that was even possible. The other side showed the real man, handsome, chiseled features, bright blue eyes, spiked blond hair and a dazzling smile. Miss P had been right about one thing: he was drop-dead gorgeous. I wondered if he had a nice ass, then rolled my eyes at myself.

I forced my attention back to the trouble at hand, letting my gaze travel casually around the casino, pausing every few seconds to focus. Anticipation and excitement shimmered off the throng like a mirage off hot asphalt. Players filed out of restaurants, gathering in rings around the tables, cheering or groaning as they rode the Lady Luck rollercoaster. Music thumped amping up the energy level, and alcohol flowed fueling the fire. The night was young but hitting its stride.

As I scanned the room, the sense that something was out of kilter grew stronger. I knew something was wrong. I could feel it. I just didn't know what. My plans to wrap this evening up quickly then head home for some shut-eye were already on the skids, so I took a deep breath and settled in to watch.

So, that's how I found myself standing outside the theater in a hotel that wasn't mine watching staff that wasn't my responsibility. Leaning against the wall next to the double doors leading into the theater, I crossed my arms and focused.

I caught trouble on my second pass.

Blonde, thin to the ragged edges of an eating disorder, hollow-eyed, underdressed, under-fed, the cocktail server was the only inert object in a sea of movement.

Normally, at this time of night, the waitresses ran to keep up with demand—the faster they moved, the more drinks they served, the more money they made... pretty simple. But this one acted like she hadn't gotten that memo. So, either she was wound tight on some mind-altering substance and not my problem, or she was up to something, which technically wasn't my problem either... although, I never had figured out how to resist tangling with one when I stumbled across it.

As I watched, the gal tucked herself in next to a wide pillar. She held her tray down at her side, which was also unusual as the wait staff used those trays like portable desks, carrying napkins, pens, notepads, little cups of olives, lemons, cherries and the like. Narrowing my eyes, I looked at her more closely. Her uniform wasn't exactly like the others, close enough not to draw attention, but different enough to raise a question. Frankly, I was surprised one of the floor managers hadn't spied her as a fake already.

40

Caught in a quandary since this wasn't my territory, I mulled over an appropriate course of action. She wasn't really doing anything that I could tell. But she was just... wrong. And even a little bit of wrong could lead to a whole bunch of worse.

What...or who... was she waiting for? And why?

With a jolting bang as someone hit the opening bar on the other side, the theater door next to me flew outward, squealing on un-oiled hinges. I raised my hand just in time to prevent being smacked in the face, as a body hurtled through. Grabbing the edge before the door could spring closed, I held it in front of me like a shield. And, at six-foot flat-footed with a tailback's ass, I needed the entire door to hide me from view. I peeked around the edge.

A few strides into the casino, the man paused, then, spying his target, launched off at an awkward gait as if he was forcing himself to slow down, act casual.

He made a beeline for the girl I'd noticed before.

From behind him, I couldn't see his features. Something about him tugged at an old, buried memory. His shoes were scuffed and his pants too short. A wrinkled overcoat with stains across the back as if he made sitting in dirty places a habit shrouded the rest of him but he had that tall man's affect—hunched shoulders, hands stuffed in his pockets, he lowered his head as if trying to blend in with a shorter world.

<u>Who was he?</u> My brain, muddled with fatigue wasn't

41

exactly leaping to help. He glanced furtively over his shoulder. Instinctively I ducked back behind the door. His face kick-started my brain.

Sticky Barnes.

So nicknamed because he had a habit of purloining valuables from their rightful owners. Usually his sort wandering through a casino triggered all sorts of attention. I eased one eye into the open to take a visual, this time scanning the casino. I doubted the Flamingo had updated its security system to incorporate the latest face-recognition stuff—it was expensive and new. So, Security probably hadn't a clue Sticky was lurking on property.

I reached for my push-to-talk. Grabbing it from its holster at my hip, I hit a familiar speed-dial.

Jerry, the Babylon's head of Security answered as if he'd been anticipating my ping. "Lucky, girl, what's up?" He sounded relaxed and nonchalant—not having any guests on-property yet certainly cut way down on his workload, and thus his stress level.

I envied him—mine was spiking, along with my blood pressure. I lowered my voice. "I'm at the Flamingo. Something's going down. Sticky Barnes is lurking and I think he's got an accomplice. Can you call over to here and get Security to send a team to the casino near the theater? Make sure they act as if it's just a normal swing through the casino. Sticky's got something up his sleeve, I'm sure of it, but I'm only going on gut here. I need time for him to show his hand."

Jerry's tone hardened. "I'm on it."

"Be sure to tell them to be subtle."

"Understood." Jerry and I went way back—we handled different sides of the same problems—so I didn't have to explain.

I reholstered my Nextel. Shifting my attention fully back to Sticky, I watched as he approached the girl. As twitchy as a rabbit out in the open, she cowered as Sticky moved in. Using his size to intimidate, he hung over her like a vulture eyeing carrion.

My eyes flicked to the far side of the casino as a Security team, stepped into the crowd. They looked too intent, muscling through with purpose. Come on Jerry. Sticky needed time to show his hand. If they grabbed him now, without probable cause, all they could do was escort him off-property.

Sticky reached out and grabbed the girl's arm. She flinched but he held her tight, pulling her against him. He glanced around, his eyes probing as he eased his other hand out of his pocket. I tried to make myself small—an impossibility—as I scrunched behind the door, wishing it was larger. His gaze came closer. I held my breath and pulled back.

Just as his eyes slithered my direction, a couple drifted out of the theater through the open doorway.

The woman clutched at her date's arm, tugging him to a stop. She pulled him around to face her. "Why do we have

43

to go, honey? The show is amazing. Come on, please!" Her voice was a high-pitched whine.

I glanced through them. Sticky's gaze brushed the couple then kept moving. I let my breath out slowly.

"Why'd you have to tell me she is guy wearing a dress?" The man growled as color flushed his cheeks a deep pink.

The woman giggled as she clutched his arm to her and sidled in next to him. "It was funny. You thought he was so hot."

The man caught me looking. I tried to keep my expression bland, but I'm sure the hint of a smile flashed across my face as my focus stayed over his shoulder on Sticky and the girl. The man shrugged as his shoulders unbunched, the fight leaving him. Then he flashed a lopsided grin. "She is really hot."

"He is hot." The woman giggled again—I wish she'd stop. "And he's makin' me horny."

That got her date's attention, and his complicity. The couple drifted back into the theater.

After that things got a bit muddled.

The Security team kept pushing through the crowd, drawing closer and closer. Sticky pulled his hand out of his pocket. I saw the flash of gold. I let the door swing shut and stepped into the open. A message sounded over the Security team's walkie-talkies, so loud you'd think the things had been set on the bullhorn setting.

44

So much for subtle.

Sticky crammed his hand back in his pocket. He whirled. His eyes caught mine. Recognition flared. Time stopped for a fraction of a heartbeat.

Then he took off at a dead run.

I was a step slower.

The girl, her eyes wide, remained glued to her spot as if wearing cement shoes, which probably would be her eventual fate if she kept hanging with bottom-feeders. Passing her, I broke stride to shout to Security to hang onto her until I got back.

One of the guards nodded. Then I put my head down and ran. Footsteps pounded behind me. I glanced quickly. The other guard was two steps behind, his gun at the ready, which didn't make me feel all that great considering it was pointed in my general direction.

I hoped like hell he still had the safety on.

Having to dodge and dart his way through the crowd slowed Sticky down. One wild-eyed glance over his shoulder and he could see I was quickly closing the gap, with the Security guard and his gun hot on my heels.

My breath rasped through my throat, hot and dry, scuffing skin like sandpaper. My chest tightened. My vision tunneled. Almost there. One step closer.

I lunged for a piece of Sticky's coat that billowed behind him as he ran.

Like a gazelle sensing the lion's pounce, Sticky darted sideways.

My hand brushed fabric. I skidded then twisted to follow him.

As I turned, Sticky pulled the bauble from his pocket. Turning, he backpedaled as he heaved it over my head. Then he turned and ran.

I braked, letting him go as I tracked the flight of the necklace arcing over the crowd.

The guard sidestepped around me, then stopped.

Without taking my eyes off the necklace as it unfurled and soared over the crowd, sparkling as the gems fractured the light, I motioned the guard on. "Get him. I'll go after that."

He gave me a quick nod and did as I said, and I raced after the necklace.

I marked where it fell into the crowd.

Within seconds I arrived in front of a man as he bent to retrieve the necklace from the floor. Blood leaking from a cut on his cheek, a confused expression on his face, the man stared at the bauble in his hand as he straightened. He didn't pocket it. He didn't try to hide the riches he held. He didn't try to jackrabbit. An honest man. Amazing.

"Are you okay?" I worked to catch my breath and calm my staccato heartbeat.

He looked up at me with the most perfect emerald eyes. Then he grinned. "Not every day you get hit with a fortune in emeralds."

46

I batted the verbal volley back. "They match your eyes."

A woman stepped in next to him. Grabbing his arm in a possessive show, she raised her eyebrows at me then turned her attention to him. "Honey, are you all right?"

"Sure," he growled as if her question was an insult to his manhood. His eyes never wavered from mine. "Are these real?" He proffered the necklace, which was indeed encrusted in huge, deep emeralds—more than I'd caught with a quick first glance.

Knowing Sticky, I figured they were. And I'd seen that necklace before. "Not sure, but I think so. If you give them to me, I can get them back to their rightful owner."

Doubt flickered across those emerald pools. "Shouldn't I give these to the cops or something?"

I reached for one of my cards I kept stuffed in the holster of my Nextel. Bent in several places, it wasn't the most reassuring evidence of my trustworthiness, but it was all I had. I thrust it at the man with the necklace. "I'm Lucky O'Toole. I work for..."

A grin split his face. "I deal Blackjack at the Mirage. I thought I recognized you—you can take this from here." He dropped the necklace in my open palm. "Emeralds are supposed to be lucky." He gave me an interesting look, one I couldn't read. "Are you feeling lucky?"

I shrugged. "So far so good."

Now, to see that man in the dress. If Miss P was right,

and I scored some hot entertainment—for the Babylon—then my luck would be right on track.

#

The late show was well under way when I eased through the door. Waving the usher off, I stepped to the side while my eyes adjusted to the darkness. The theater was packed, not an empty seat. The band played the intro to a Cher song—I recognized the tune but couldn't name it. The set pieces were actually simpler than I imagined. They framed the stage where the spotlights focused on The Great Teddie Divine.

And the Great Teddie Divine was… divine. I'd watched enough entertainers in my relatively short time on this planet to know the real deal when I saw it. Amazingly, Miss P had been spot-on.

Even sheathed in sequins, and balancing on impossible heels, Teddie Divine oozed charisma as he sashayed across the stage channeling Cher. He clearly loved playing to the audience. Milking every movement, every note, he became Cher. His voice, velvety smooth sultry heat, held the crowd in a spell worthy of Mesmer. Cher couldn't have done it better. I kept having to remind myself that I was watching a guy in a dress.

Finally, I quit fighting it. I leaned back holding up the wall as I let Teddie and his show carry me away.

The Big Boss was going to have a cow.

#

It took an hour for the crowd in Teddie's dressing room to clear of fans and for me to shoulder my way through the handlers to the front for an audience. He'd changed. The woman had disappeared. In her place stood one of the handsomest men I'd laid my eyes on…ever. Spiky blond hair, blue eyes, a wicked grin that turned the blue of his eyes all deep and sensual, he'd donned a Harvard sweatshirt and jeans just tight enough to show off the stellar ass I'd suspected.

If he was straight, which I seriously doubted, he would be trouble, big trouble.

I stepped in front of him. His eyes met mine. Words fled as rational thought dissipated like smoke in a strong wind. I held my hand out toward him, gold and emeralds dripping trough my splayed fingers.

With a raised eyebrow and a slanting smile, he held my eyes for a moment, then glanced down. When his eyes found mine again, questions had replaced the playfulness, and the color of his eyes had deepened.

Under his piercing gaze, I felt a blush color my cheeks and another sort of warmth flood through me. "I believe this is yours," I stammered.

A quick shake of his head. "A cheap copy. I just put the real one in the safe. But I appreciate its return from… ?"

Oh god, his voice was liquid honey. I took a deep

breath and tried to quell my rising libido. Could he be straight? Oh God, could he? I glanced over his shoulder at the photos on his dressing table. One of his mom, perhaps, but that was all. Buoyed on my rising libido, my spirits soared. Thoughts pinged in my head like random lottery balls in a spinning cage. "From one of our more successful jewel thieves. I'd say the one you locked up is the fake."

"The necklace is on loan. It's insured, but still... " His face blanched. "The deductible is huge."

"Not a worry now, then." Somehow I managed to sound somewhat cavalier.

The serious fled from his baby blues. "Thank you for that. Could you tell me how you came to be in possession of my jewels?"

I bit my lip for a moment, not trusting myself to give him a straight answer. I scanned his face. If he was flirting he hid it well, so I pulled myself together as best I could.

I introduced myself... he didn't make a smart comment about my name which made me like him—of course, I was already so inclined—then I told him the whole scenario, as much as I could remember given my mission of mercy had turned into thoughts of an entirely different kind of ... mission. Christ, Lucky, pull yourself together. What's the matter with you? A bead of sweat trickled between my breasts. And I felt that long absent pang of instant, wicked attraction.

Teddie mulled my story then turned and bent to retrieve the other necklace from the safe giving me an

50

unobstructed view of his ass. I tried to keep myself together, but failed. Of course the fact that my sex life, such as it was, had been sacrificed, along with my sanity, on the altar of twenty-hour workdays didn't help matters. He weighed the two necklaces—the real one and the fake—one in each hand. He turned and looked up at me stopping my heart. "You're right. You had the real one. You've saved my ass. I don't know how I can repay you."

"I want you." The words were out of my mouth and hanging in the air between us before I knew what had happened.

Teddie bolted upright as if hit with a Taser, then whirled to face me. "What?"

Opening and closing my mouth, I probably looked like a guppy, I decided to just forge ahead—trying to make this better would just make it worse. Trust me on that one. I know myself pretty well. "I want you." I started to explain about the Babylon and the show and all of that, but stopped dead when I ran into Teddie's burgeoning smile.

"Do you always get what you want?" he asked, not even trying to hide the flirt.

I smiled. Or maybe it's more accurate to say I grinned like an idiot. Then I shrugged. "I'm lucky that way."

THE END

Le Petit Mort

By Sheryl Greenblatt

Leila stood in front of the Gentleman's Club, just a few hundred feet from the famed Las Vegas Strip, and took a deep breath. The large building stood, covered in blinking lights and fake leaves, a symbol of everything that had gone wrong in her life. She stared at the fluorescent sign in the blacked out windows advertising that they were "Proudly Serving the NRA". She thought she'd left that behind when she got the hell out of Texas. Leila licked her lips and tried to summon up some saliva. Her mouth was dry, like she'd gotten rid of her tooth brush and replaced it with a sheep.

She tightened her grip around the backpack with her "uniform" in it. Despite the lack of fabric, the bag seemed to weigh about 100 pounds. "Come on, Leila. You've got to do this," she said to herself. Two weeks in this city and she was down to her last five dollars and out of restaurants to apply to. She supposed she should be grateful to Big Benny, the club's owner who was willing to consider a month of pole dancing classes, purchased through a local deal website when she turned 18, as "experience." She took another deep breath and gripped the door handle tightly. A whoosh of cold air hit her as she opened the door and stepped into the gaudy red hallway. She looked around her. Floor to ceiling red velour. It was like walking into a vagina. A bouncer stepped out in front of her and ran his gaze up her body.

"You the new dancer?" He did his best to fold his beefy arms across his chest, but his pecs got in the way and he looked more like he was trying to carry an imaginary basketball.

She nodded, trying to infuse her voice with cheer that wasn't there. "I'm Leila. Is Big Benny in?"

The bouncer nodded his head, a vein bulging in his neck with every downward movement. He pointed to a small door to his left. "He's in his office." His eyes traveled to the skin peeking out of her blouse. "Can't wait to see you dance." His lips spread into a smile that made Leila cross her own arms and cover up that bit of skin, but she knew it was a waste. *Better get used to this now. The customers aren't coming to hear me discuss Tolstoy.* She walked through the door and stood in a concrete hallway. Ugly, but still a welcome break from the reproductive system she walked into. She trudged towards a gray door at the end of the hall. The door held an outline of a penis with "Big Benny" written inside it. She closed her eyes and pretended that she hadn't fought with her father about college, that she'd never left home. But when she opened them, there was the penis. She lifted her hand to knock on the door but jumped back when it opened before she

54

made contact.

Big Benny stood in the doorway, all 4 foot 11 inches of him, a black fedora tilted to the side of his tiny head. Irony at its finest, Leila had thought when she came for the "interview."

He stepped aside and waved towards the couch.

"Come in to my office."

"Said the spider to the fly," Leila mumbled.

"What was that, dear?"

"I said I'd sure like to try."

Big Benny closed the door behind her and coughed. A thick wet sound that he followed up with another drag of a cigar. It was almost as big as him. He pointed to a bank of television screens beside his desk, a live feed to every room in the club, including the dressing room next door. Leila shuddered.

"Candy's going to show you the ropes," he said, but his gaze lingered on the redhead undressing on camera. He pressed a red button on his desk and spoke into a microphone. "Candy, my sweet girl, come show our newest gal around."

The redhead glanced towards the camera and gave the thumbs up. She took one more look in the mirror, pursing red lips and then disappeared out of view. Leila's hands trembled slightly and she swallowed hard. Her mouth was no longer dry and she swallowed again to keep the spit under control.

"I don't believe in paying taxes, so paperwork's pretty easy here." Big Benny slid a single sheet across his desk and dropped a pen on top of it. Leila picked up the pen, the Pin-Up girl on the barrel lost her shirt as she clicked the top. She glanced at the form, the words swimming before her eyes. She read something about not suing for sexual harassment by the clientele or the staff. With a small shake of her head, she lifted the naked woman and scrawled her signature across the line. Maybe she'd use "Rock Bottom" as her new stripper name.

Candy bounced into the room, cherry red lips and beach ball sized breasts covered in a candy bra, entering several seconds before the rest of her materialized. "You must be Leila." She wrapped her arms around Leila and squeezed. Leila had no time to breathe and feared that the last sight she would see was monstrous boobs.

Big Benny placed a hand on Candy's shoulder. "Let's give Leila some room to breathe. Not everyone likes to be suffocated in your titties."

The redhead giggled and loosened her grip. "I've got her from here," she said to Benny and then turned to Leila. "You're in good hands." She grabbed Leila from her chair and dragged her from the room. Leila thought about digging her heels in, but the growl in her stomach reminded her that her next meal would only come *after* she'd earned some tips. She swallowed another round of spit, and her pride, and followed the human blow up doll out of the office.

Candy ushered her into the dressing room, where several women were now lounging around. Fishnet clad legs rested atop mirrored vanities, a joint traveling between several of the women.

"You can get ready in here." She pointed towards the camera and waved. "Big Benny likes to watch. Sometimes if you put on a show when you get changed, he throws a few extra bucks in your pay envelope." She shook her ass a bit to illustrate her point. Leila's stomach soured. "Why don't you get changed and we'll finish the tour?"

Leila dropped her backpack on the floor and pulled out the black, patent leather bra and panty set she'd spent her last few dollars on. Her "investment" as she'd taken to calling it. She slipped out of her clothing, her back to the camera, and shimmied into the outfit. It was going to take some time to get used to having a voyeur as a boss. It made her yearn for the manic-depressive she'd worked under at her previous waitressing job. She hooked the buckles on the Fuck-me shoes she'd purchased on a dare after high school and started to touch up her makeup.

Candy's face appeared in the mirror beside her. "Honey, don't put too much effort into your makeup there. It's not like they have brains."

Leila forced a chuckle. "They have brains, they just keep them in their pants."

Candy patted her on the back. "Those don't always stay in their pants."

What have I gotten myself into?

Candy grabbed Leila by the arm and led her out of the dressing room. "Now let's get you out there and see what you can do."

Leila allowed herself to be led behind the stage but froze when Candy pushed her up the stairs. "Give it your all honey, and remember that Big Benny is always watching." She shouted something to the DJ and Leila cringed as Eric Clapton pumped through the sound system.

The DJ leaned his lips towards the microphone. "Let's give a warm La Petit Mort welcome to our new gal, Leila!" A slow, weak clap traveled through the audience. She felt another push from behind and hoped for the first time that a brain embolism like the one that had taken her mother so many years ago, would finish her off. She was out of luck and her shoes were fully on the stage. She looked out across the audience, but the spotlight prevented her from seeing the crowd before her. All she could see was the shiny pole in the center of the stage. She conjured up memories of those fitness classes, the ones where the instructor sarcastically nicknamed her "Grace" and announced to the class that she had "Oh shit grip" on the pole. Time to prove that bitchy instructor, and her father wrong.

Leila picked up speed as she strutted across the stage, a peacock showing off its feathers for the first time. She grabbed the pole, slipped a leg around it and twirled. The metal nipped at her skin as she fought to stay upright. Losing her balance, she attempted to make the fall look purposeful and landed on all fours, just as Mr. Clapton sang "Got me on my knees". She flung her neck around, sending her hair flying in all directions like Tawny Kitaen in a Whitesnake video. The audience began a low howl and she rolled over on her back, legs kicking up in a "V."

The rest of the song went by in a blur and Candy waited just off stage with a bottle of water and a big grin. She slapped Leila on the back. "Great job. I've already got a lap dance lined up for you." She unscrewed the bottle cap and handed the water over. "That's where we make our real money."

Leila gulped down the bottle as if she'd never had a drink before. She vowed never to mock pole dancers again. Every part of her body hurt. No need for a gym membership. She glanced around the room, the spotlight no longer blinding her eyes, and gasped. The "clientele" moved slowly. Tattered clothing hung off withered bodies and graying skin.

"What the fuck?" she exclaimed.

Candy stopped in place. "Big Benny didn't tell you did, he?"

Leila stood, eyes wide and locked on one particular man, leg resting on a table, a bone protruding from underneath his ripped pants.

"Fucking zombies!"

"Shhh!" Candy warned. "They don't like the term '*zombies*'." She held her fingers up in air quotes. "Big

59

Benny likes to call them the Newly Re-Animated."

Leila flashed back to the NRA sign in the window. It now made perfect sense why her Charlton Heston comment during her interview was met with an awkward, confused chuckle. Well, nothing about this situation made perfect sense. But she supposed that cleared up one question.

"We dance for fucking zombies." Leila shook her head and stared up the ceiling. God, she should've listened to her father and gone to law school when she had the chance. *But I want to travel the world,* she'd told him. She was a fucking idiot.

Candy clasped a hand over her mouth. "Stop using the Z word. After they started outnumbering the living customer base, Benny said we had to evolve or die." She looked out over the crowd. "They aren't so bad."

One of the other dancers screamed as a "customer" jumped onto her back and took a bite out of her shoulder. The burly security guard from the front door was on him in seconds, ripping his head off of his body and throwing him to the ground. A few of the other dancers gathered around the victim and ushered her into the back, plucking teeth out of her shoulder and stroking her hair for comfort.

"Bruno is great, we only lose one or two girls a month since he started." She pointed to a curtained off area towards the back. "They are better tippers than you'd expect." She nodded her head and began to walk towards the curtain, offering a small wave to Leila. "Come on, the first one is always the hardest."

Leila choked back a mixture of tears and disgust, but she followed Candy. Her edible bra and panties were made with the same candy Leila had as necklaces at her 10th birthday party. The tears were subsiding but the self loathing still flowed freely.

Candy pulled the red curtain back and pointed to two NRAs on the couch. "Which one do you want?" she whispered into Leila's ear. Leila's gaze traveled between the two walking corpses. Both had patches of hair missing, sunken in eye sockets and cracked, blackened teeth. "Oh sweet Jesus," she whispered.

"Just take the one on the left. He's a new customer, probably smells a bit better." Candy dropped her hand and strode toward the man on the right, flinging a leg over his shoulder to rest on the bench backing. She gyrated, pushing her pelvis towards his face. He laughed, a tooth escaping from his mouth and bouncing off her thigh.

Leila's customer stared at her. She stared back, frozen in place. A slap on her ass woke her from her shock induced daze. Big Benny stood behind her, looking up. "Go get him, Leila. If you can't do this, there's 20 more women where you came from."

She crossed her arms over her breasts, the metal studs from her bra poking into her flesh. "No," she said to Benny, "I can do it."

She stepped, taking her sweet time over to the couch.

61

Candy was in full lap dance mode, rubbing her breasts in the zombie's face while he tried to bite off pieces of candy... or flesh. Leila wasn't sure at this point.

"Boobs!" He yelled in between dry, crackling laughs that sent shivers down Leila's spine.

She fought the chills that wracked her body and nodded at her own customer. She turned around, beginning with some ass swinging. Maybe it would be easier if she couldn't see him. She heard groans, of what she assumed was pleasure, as she moved her ass in circles in front of him. He put a hand on her hips and tried to guide them, but she whirled around and his arm ripped out of its socket, the hand still gripping her body.

Leila froze, screaming, and stared at the arm. The customer didn't seem the least bit phased. She kept screaming.

Candy stopped mid-wiggle and placed a hand on Leila's shoulder. "Calm down," she mouthed and yanked the arm off of Leila's hip. She held it up, wagging it at Leila's customer. "Hands off!" and then tossed it behind the couch. Leila watched it travel through the air. It landed in a pile of other body parts, flies dancing around the heap like an all you can eat buffet. She let out a small whimper. Her customer nodded his head to the music and smiled, a tooth plopping into his Jack and Coke.

"Keep dancing!" Candy yelled. "He's really into it!"

How could she tell? Leila wondered. He still had the same blank, my-face-is-melting, expression that he'd had when she started. She began to dance again, but she couldn't tear her eyes away from the loosely hanging t-shirt sleeve where his arm had previously been. Transfixed and nauseated, she looked up to the ceiling and tried to ignore the travesty of nature before her. The song came to an end and the customer reached into his pocket and pulled out a wad of cash. Leila allowed a small smile to spread across her lips as she reached for the money. She closed her hand around it, feeling his leathery hand inside her own. *Just a few more seconds*, she promised herself and drew her hand away from his.

She glanced down to examine her spoils and found his thumb sitting amongst the bills. Terror rocked through her body and she turned towards the curtain and ran. Big Benny was on the other side of the red velour, his face molded in a big, waxy smile. "Good job, Leila. I knew you were the right gal for the job."

Her elbow collided with the little man's shoulder and sent him sailing into an occupied table. She glanced behind her in time to see body parts fly in different directions like pins in a morbid bowling game.

"You'll never work in this town again!" Big Benny yelled after her. She held up a hand. That was just fine with her. Grabbing her things from the dressing room, she ran into the hot night air, still wearing nothing but her "uniform", and scrambled to locate her cell phone. She dialed the number and let out a breath when the man answered.

"Daddy, I'm so sorry. I'm coming home."

Discretion a Must

By Lindsay Wright

Even his clothes were ripe with the stench of his defeat. They stank of cigarette smoke and nervous sweat from too many hours at poker tables. His wallet contained a twenty and a single condom, three years past its expiration date. The only saving grace he could think of was that his motel room was paid in full until the end of the week.

Victor chucked his dog-eared poker books into the trash can.

Time for Plan B.

He pawned his guitar and the watch his ex-girlfriend gave him as a birthday gift years ago. Outside the pawn shop, a man crossing in front of him dropped a hundred onto the sidewalk. Victor's mouth watered at the sight of the lone bill abandoned on the concrete.

Without thinking, he flagged down the man. "I think you dropped this."

Victor retreated to the motel, his head slumped between his shoulders and his hands thrust into the pockets of jeans. *Stupid, stupid, stupid.* The pawn proceeds that

65

thickened his wallet did little to console him over the loss of the hundred dollars he could have had.

As he stepped into his room, the crunch of paper under his shoe pulled him from his bitter thoughts. He read the folded page, a photo-copied message with faded letters and a simple design.

Help wanted! $500 a week. Discretion a must.

At the bottom, a hand-written note. *We have an opportunity for you, Victor. Please call.*

Victor surveyed the line of doors spanning either direction of his room. He didn't see any other folded papers under them, but perhaps the other occupants already threw away the message.

He scoffed and crumbled the page in his fist, molding it like a snowball before tossing it at the trash bin. It bounced off the rim and landed near a heap of clothes.

For several days, the jigsaw puzzles from home and hours of game shows kept him from the casinos. His hunger forced him from the safety of his room. At the grocery store, one-armed bandits accosted him with blinking lights and beckoning jingles as soon as he passed through the doors.

Two hours later, Victor blinked and saw that outside the store, day fell to night and his pawn proceeds shriveled to twenty-four dollars. A cold sweat prickled his forehead and dripped down his temples. He sat for a moment, frozen with panic, and after a moment, collected himself enough to shuffle through the aisles for food.

By the time the balled-up job offer resurfaced, he had nine dollars to his name and another four days left on his motel room. The wad of paper fell from the bundle of clothes as he dumped it into a washing machine at the laundromat. Clean clothes were a luxury he wasn't sure he could afford, but then there was the offer, in black and white in front of him.

"Opportunity, my ass," Victor mumbled as he re-read the note. He paused. Plan C was either selling a kidney on the black market or prostituting himself.

He dialed the number.

A young woman answered. "Hello?"

Victor stammered something about a wrong number.

"Wait," she said. "Are you Victor?" He paused, his mouth open. "You got the right number. You want a job?"

"What kind of job?"His voice sounded shrill and the words felt misshapen in his mouth.

"Meet me at the coffee shop on the corner by your motel in an hour," she said.

Images of his bloody body lying bent in some dark alley passed his mind's eye like a macabre slideshow, but he finished his laundry and went to the coffee shop. He couldn't decide if the gnawing in his stomach was hunger or anxiety or both.

Victor didn't even have time to attempt the newspaper crossword puzzle before she approached him. He was locked in her gaze, trapped, and he gulped back his dread and looked up at her. Blonde, mid-twenties, in jeans and a t-shirt. He

67

wouldn't even have noticed her if it weren't for the fact that she stood over him, blocking his view of the cuter, perkier blonde behind the counter.

"Victor." She didn't smile.

He nodded. She introduced herself as Nellie and sat and explained the job to him. He never learned her last name, or the name of the company, only that his sole duty would be to deliver packages to addresses across the city.

Nellie glared at him with warning. "Look, the job is simple," she said. "But–" she held up a finger and shook it at him like she was scolding a child—"Do not open the boxes under any circumstances. You got it?"

"Is this illegal?" Victor cocked his head at her and narrowed his eyes.

She rolled hers and mumbled something under her breath. "Just don't open the packages."

"Fine. I get it. How did you know who I am?"

Nellie smirked. "It's my job to know things."

She never asked if he had a car or requested identification or proof of anything. She only gave directions, a list of addresses, and the packages he was to deliver.

The first delivery was a long rectangular chunk of cardboard with a name written on it in black marker. The woman who opened the door peeked at Victor through the screen and as soon as she saw what was in his hands, her

68

eyes widened and she opened the door.

"I have a delivery for you." His script.

"Thank you," she said in an accent he couldn't place. Her hands trembled as she took the box from him. She nodded thanks, nodded and nodded as she closed the screen door and stumbled back into the house in a trance-like stupor. She rattled something in a foreign language, speaking to herself, or someone else he couldn't see.

Victor frowned and rapped his fingers onto the steering wheel of his car as he thought. Nellie warned him that what he delivered was "personal and private". *Sex toys? Drugs? Pornography? Ill-gotten gains? Blackmail material?*

He drove all over the valley, to trailer parks in Sunrise Manor and track home developments in Summerlin. The homes, the neighborhoods, and the faces of the people— these details floated around his brain like pieces of a jigsaw puzzle that he tried to snap into place.

Nellie paid him five hundred in cash once a week whether he made one delivery or four. The job paid ample for the effort it required and left him plenty of time to look for another job, but Victor, against his own nagging judgment, remained inert.

Each night he slurped ramen noodles out of the motel coffee pot and considered quitting. He lay on top of the scratchy bedspread and recalled the expressions of the week.

The woman whose mascara made black trails down her cheeks as she gulped back tears. A teen boy with a cigarette dripping from his lips received a box so large that Victor almost couldn't fit it in the backseat of his car.

"Oh, wow," said the boy. "Shit, man." He cleared his throat and scratched at his head, stubbing his cigarette out on the door frame as he glanced down the hallway behind him. The boy snatched the package and hunched over it, shielding it with his body, scurrying clumsily up the stairs and out of sight.

Victor shook each package, listening to its sound, guessing its contents the way children do with Christmas gifts. His divergent customers never granted him any revelations. They shut doors in his face, gave him looks of thanks or embarrassment, looks that he read as go away, leave.

"Oh, it's you," said one man when he saw Victor on his porch. He shifted his feet to corral his two barking dogs and then held out his arms. "I'll take that now."

Victor squinted and handed over the heavy tool-box-sounding package. "How—how did you know–?"

"Have a good day." The man smiled as he shut and locked the door.

"This might be a crazy question," Victor said to Nellie one night as he met her in the parking lot of the coffee shop. "But who exactly are we working for?" He told himself he'd be reassured if he just had that one answer, that one piece of the puzzle.

70

Nellie shrugged. "The hell if I know."

Victor's voice came out a pitch higher. "You don't know? What the hell is going on?" He raked his hands through his hair, groaned, and banged a fist onto the roof of his car.

"I was approached. Just like you." She pulled an envelope stuffed with twenties out of her purse and extended it to him.

Victor took deep breaths and stared at the envelope. "These people know I'm going to be delivering a package, right? But it's not something they bought or ordered. It's something else, right?" The corner of Nellie's mouth curved into a hint of a smile. "Can't you at least answer that question?"

"All I'm authorized to give you," she said, "is this." She wagged the envelope in front of him as if it were a bone and he a yappy dog.

Victor plucked it away from her with another groan. *One more week*, he thought, even though he still had nowhere near enough cash to go home without his tail between his legs.

One more week, he told himself each week. But the five hundred he earned wasn't even enough to keep the motel roof over his head. He tried to make it grow in the casinos and occasionally met with success. Just when he got to feeling positive again, a losing hand swept it all out from under him and he crept back to his lonely motel room with a disgust so palpable that it felt like a pair of dirty clothes he couldn't take off.

The same old aura of stench led him back to Nellie in the parking lot of the coffee shop. The list of deliveries grew along with his frustration.

Victor read the name on the box—Goldman—chewed an antacid and shook the rectangular package. Mystery contents thudded and weighed next to nothing in his sweaty hands. He fingered the box cutter in his pocket, but sighed and stared ahead, to the curved driveway of the Goldman residence. A bald man in a pinstripe suit came strutting out of the house toward a convertible parked opposite Victor. A phone piece flashed blue in his ear and made him look like a humanistic cyborg.

"You Goldman?" Victor said as he approached the man.

He nodded and looked down at the object in Victor's hands. For the first time ever, the customer didn't flinch, lift his eyebrows in delight, twitch with nervousness, or even crack a grin. Victor studied his face, noted stubble and the pockmarks of old acne scars. He waited, but for the first time, someone was apathetic.

Victor shifted the box in his hands. "Uh, I have a delivery for you."

"Oh, yeah," Goldman said, remembering. Patting his pockets, he pulled out a set of keys and wielded one like a makeshift knife.

Victor pulled the box cutter from his back jeans pocket, flicked out the blade with a snap of his wrist. Goldman slit the box open like he was gutting a dead fish. He flipped up the flaps. Victor stepped closer. He glanced from the contents of the box to the man's face, back and forth, waiting.

Goldman's face fell, his mouth deepening to a frown, nostrils flaring, eyes widening.

"What is it?" Victor asked. He craned his neck to get a better view even though he knew he was being nosy.

Beads of sweat glistened on Goldman's forehead. He slowly reached into the box and cradled its contents on his fingers.

A purple ribbon, frayed and faded, lay in his hands. From a gold bar at its tip hung a round medal with a colonial face in profile.

Victor sucked in his breath. He watched the customer's face.

Goldman's chest heaved and he blinked rapidly. After a long moment of silence, he clicked a button on the ear piece and said, "Call Mom." He eyed Victor. "I had no idea," he said. "Holy sh—Mom." He squared his shoulders and covered the medal in his hands. "You'll never believe it."

Victor slunk back toward his car, but kept his eyes on Goldman. He didn't want to leave, he didn't want to miss out on what was about to happen.

The drive across town gave Victor plenty of time to

stew on his frustration. It left such a bad taste in his mouth that he spat out the window as he sat in traffic waiting for a light to turn green. Waiting. Always waiting.

He shook his head. *No.*

Next on the list: Eleanor Weatherby.

The name conjured an image of his grandmother, a frail woman shaped like a question mark. She always met Victor's eyes with hawk-like intensity and inspired his love of puzzles.

Eleanor's house was nestled in a neighborhood with cracked streets and mature trees that towered over the one story homes. Miles away, The Strip was piled high with suites bigger than these houses.

Victor parked on the street and approached the house. No car sat in the driveway. Patches of weeds grew in the dirt yard suffocated by pine needles. Paint peeled to reveal chicken wire under the stucco of the house.

He stood on the porch with the square box under his arm. He listened, his mouth dry and sweat beading on the back of his neck. Nothing but mourning doves and someone's far off ranchero music. He looked around and, satisfied that he was alone, shook the box to his ear. Clinking, like metal against glass and a liquid sloshing. Wine? No, the shape of the box was all wrong. A bottle of perfume?

He sighed and pressed the doorbell. Nothing. He pressed again and this time listened for the chime. Shifting the package to his other arm, he knocked on the metal security gate in front of the door. He knocked harder, banging it against its frame.

The door creaked open and Victor lowered his gaze to meet that of Eleanor Weatherby. She was several feet shorter than he, and fiercer, more weathered than his long-deceased grandmother.

"Yes?" she gasped in a sing-songy voice.

"I have a delivery for you." He held up the box. More metallic clinking from inside as he handled it.

"Oh, yes!" She dusted her hands on the hem of her long cardigan. She cracked the door wider and propped the screen door open with her foot.

He wedged himself between the doors and stretched his arms toward her, but as she reached out to take the package from him, he let go.

The box bounced off the metal grating of the door frame and landed on its side on the concrete stoop. A louder clink and the sound of glass breaking accompanied its landing.

Eleanor gasped and Victor bent to retrieve the box. "I'm so sorry," he said. He winced at his own insincerity. His heart galloped with anticipation even while he knew his contrite words were hollow and slightly giddy. "I think something broke. Do you mind if I--?"

She gaped at him with wide eyes, her mouth open in a silent cry.

A bristle of guilt made him frown. "I'm going to... it's broken glass. I don't want you to cut yourself."

She led him to her kitchen where he set the box on the counter. Liquid darkened one corner of it. Victor cut the top open and carefully retrieved the pieces inside. He set them one by one onto the counter for Eleanor to see.

First, the thin and rounded pieces of glass. Bits of white plastic snow clung to them. "I can try to glue that back together for you," he told her, even though he suspected it would be impossible. *Damnit.* Doubt coupled with the existing guilt made his quest for answers seem silly, childish even.

The base of the snow globe was yellow and in pink slanted script read one word: Hawaii. A little metal pole stood in the middle of the base and tied to it were two tarnished rings of different sizes. They dangled by a strand of clear fishing line.

Eleanor choked out a cry and covered her mouth with her hands. Tears formed in the corners of her eyes.

"Bernie," she said and began rifling through the kitchen drawers.

"Ma'am?" said Victor.

"Scissors."

Victor slid the fishing line against the blade of his box cutter and freed the two rings. He cupped them in his open palm. Eleanor slid the smaller ring onto her finger, tears flowing down her cheeks. The wrinkles on her face were like rivulets through which they drained.

She clasped the larger ring to her chest and looked up at the ceiling. "Bernie."

76

"Bernie?"

She met Victor's eyes. "I never wanted to give these up," she said. She slipped the ring onto her thumb but it hung there lopsided.

"Some people wear them on necklaces," Victor said.

"We went to Hawaii on our honeymoon."

He unclasped his own thin gold chain and slid the ring—Bernie's ring—onto the chain before clasping it around Eleanor's neck.

"How did you know?" She sniffled.

"I don't know anything," he said.

Her chin trembled. Victor frowned.

"I wanted to get them back, but I couldn't."

He nodded. "It's okay, ma'am. I know exactly what you mean." He thought of his guitar and watch and the fact that they just might be lost to him forever.

An idea—perhaps the answer—formed in his brain, as clear as the broken shards of glass on Eleanor's counter. Other questions remained, but for now, they could wait. He slid his arm around Eleanor's back and gave her a little pat. She leaned onto his shoulder and sobbed.

"It's okay," he said, over and over again.

When he returned to his motel room that night, he spread the pages of the newspaper's classified section across the bed and bent over them, pen poised in his fingers. He circled the cheapest apartments listed and then sat back and surveyed the sea of tiny print in front of him. A sense of relief relaxed his shoulders for the first time since he arrived in Vegas.

Back home, everyone told him he was foolish to escape to Vegas. He admitted it might be naïve to seek transformation there, as so many had done before him. Yet he arrived hopeful, with the exhaust-filled air of downtown in his lungs like some magical elixir. It wasn't long before he surrendered to disillusion, but now, now he could relax. The answers weren't hidden in a deck of cards, but he had discretion to spare.

The Dream Emporium

By Jessica Cline

When Will Davis folded his long legs into the backseat of the cab, James took one look at him in the rearview and plugged the destination into his GPS. Only a certain kind of person heads to 37 Cameron Street at 10 pm on a Saturday night. After 26 years of driving cabs in Las Vegas, James Gunning could pick them out before they even had their hand on the door. The guy at the blackjack table on a streak so hot it came with a key to a luxury suite and lobster dinner; the woman sauntering through the night club smelling of jasmine and desire, alight with the knowledge that she was only an alluring smile from anything she wanted; tech entrepreneurs turned tiny gods for the weekend—not them. Not even close. Thirty-seven Cameron people were the people who watched the weekend high rollers from the nickel slots and prayed that the jasmine-scented woman would turn her alluring smile on them.

People like Will Davis.

Will was in his mid twenties with sandy hair and

pleasant features and might have been more remarkable with some confidence and a better haircut. But it wasn't the hair that tipped him off to this kid's destination. It was the wanting so thick around him it took up a physical space, like a second passenger in the car.

"Where ya headed?" James asked, not that he needed to.

"Hang on, I've got the address here," Will said. He fumbled in the pocket of his jeans and emerged triumphant with a folded slip of paper he handed to James. "The concierge wouldn't say much about it. He said it was something I should find out about for myself."

James just smiled a knowing smile and set out on the familiar route. This would be a one-way trip, and someone else was paying the fare.

***

Will's expression darkened as they rolled to a stop about twenty-five feet from a series of nondescript warehouses in the shadow of the Strip.

He rolled a single matchstick over his knuckles as he surveyed his destination. This was not exactly what he'd envisioned when he'd asked the concierge for "something more" than the typical Vegas experience. The only thing to mark the place as anything more than another nameless warehouse was the blue neon sign above the double doors. It buzzed to life unselfconscious in its tackiness: The Dream

Emporium

"Hmmm," he said. Though Will fancied himself the king of the neutral *hmmm*, able to placate disappointed customers and parents alike, this hmmm sounded less like a synonym for *Interesting* and more like a stand in for *Where the fuck did you just take me*?

Just when he was about to tell the smug cab driver to forget it and head back to his room and his drug store vodka, a female figure materialized from the darkness of a nearby alley. Will watched with renewed interest as she strode with purpose toward the Emporium's door. Though bleached of color by the streetlights, the impossible evening gown she wore shimmered over her curves as she moved. There was an ethereal quality to her something that made her seem more smoke and mirrors than flesh. Women like this didn't travel in the same social circles as Will did. Where had she come from?

Will scanned the area. No other cars were parked nearby. He hadn't seen any residential neighborhoods here in the surrounding industrial district. And this didn't exactly seem like the kind of place a beautiful woman would go for a stroll by herself after dark.

It occurred to him that he would very much like to go wherever she was headed, but because he was Will, he kept his hand poised on the door handle and observed before taking any action. The woman paused just short of the Emporium door and dipped her body forward. Will craned his neck and caught the outline of a silver drinking fountain behind

81

her silhouette. After taking a sip, she rummaged in her purse and produced an empty water bottle. She filled it, but just before she disappeared inside the mysterious warehouse, light glinted off of the bottle in her hand. Will did a double take. The deep garnet liquid inside couldn't have been water.

"You just gonna sit here all night?" The cabbie turned around in his seat and faced Will, his face a mask that could make him a rich man if he visited the poker tables. If the cabbie knew anything more about the girl and her peculiar bottle, he didn't let on. Or maybe after you'd been a cab driver in this town for so many years, you'd seen enough weird shit that nothing surprised you anymore. "Doesn't matter to me. The meter's still running."

As much as Will's weird-shit-o-meter was going off like crazy, this place had the air of something starting. Something strange, no doubt, but something far better than answering phones all day.

He stepped out into the dry desert air and hesitated. Maybe he should have a way out of here. Just in case.

"Could you, uh, wait here awhile?"

The cabbie only smiled and retrieved a rolled up magazine from the glove box.

When Will reached the entrance, he eyed the pair of drinking fountains standing sentinel beside the doors. What an odd place for a drinking fountain. An even odder place for two.

With a tentative hand, he pressed the button on the one closest to the door. Water with a metallic tang spluttered towards him. At the top of the fountain two words lit up: *Eternal Life.*

Will looked behind him, certain that he was the unwitting mark of someone trying to boost ratings on his YouTube channel. But he didn't see any cameras anywhere under the streetlights that whitewashed the night and turned the whole place into something out of a noir movie set. In the distance, the cabbie looked up briefly from his magazine, but went right back to it as though this sort of thing happened every day.

Will's curiosity won out over any potential internet embarrassment and he tried the second fountain. Dark, garnet liquid flowed from under the words *Fame and Fortune.* So she was a fame and fortune girl, he mused. Will didn't mind. He wouldn't mind having a bit of fame and fortune himself. Speaking of which... he dipped a finger into the stream and brought it to his nose. The earthy aroma of red wine filled his nostrils.

A tingling sensation sang through him at the scent, but he stepped back from the beckoning fountains. What *was* this place? He thought back to his request for "something more" and the concierge's sly smile. Though the rational part of his brain insisted this must be some kind of gimmick for bored tourists, the seductive lure of money and notoriety teased at his imagination. He pictured himself in a $3000 suit giving an interview on some Hollywood news show. He didn't really give a shit about being on TV, but girls did. Some of them, at least.

They'd follow him and cater to his every desire, just to have a piece of him to carry away and brag to their friends about. His gaze shifted to the fountain dripping with the promised elixir of life. Why stop at money when he could have lifetimes of fame and fortune? He'd be like those sparkly vampires everyone was into a few years back. Not the sparkly part, and not the creepy "I see you when you're sleeping" part, but rich and infinite. The enigmatic billionaire with the smooth skin of a nineteen year old. He'd watch the stock market, wait it out. Compound interest was no joke. He'd see every country, get his own private jet, learn how to order champagne in thirty languages. If that didn't get him laid on a regular basis, he didn't know what would.

A car horn blared. Will snapped to attention. *Jesus.*

The cabbie leaned out the window. "I'd think long and hard before taking a drink of those, son." He tapped a finger to his nose.

Will raked a hand through his hair and tried to think of a comeback while waiting for his heart to stop thumping like something out of an Edgar Allen Poe story. But *Who asked you?* and *Mind your own business* both sounded much too insolent and childish— neither of which he wanted associated with his new self— so he kept his mouth shut and kicked at a discarded condom wrapper on the sidewalk.

For an instant he considered slinking back to the cab and forgetting the whole thing. What was he doing in this old warehouse district with trick water fountains and women in furs and evening gowns anyway? He could go back to the hotel. Pass a pleasant night with a video poker machine and cocktail waitresses who had to smile at him when they brought him free booze. Come Monday, he'd go back to his sad little life. Then an image of himself, sitting at that desk as days stretched into years, assaulted him. Sitting there wasting his life away while old ladies droned on about the evils of automated menu options and drool collected under the place where he'd fallen asleep on the call center job. Was that really how he wanted to spend the rest of his days? He would *not* be that guy. He couldn't.

Will threw a glance back at the cabbie then drank defiantly. Twice.

With a swipe of his shirtsleeve, Will wiped the last traces of Fame and Fortune from his lips and entered the warehouse shop. As the headiness of his subversive act enveloped him, he couldn't stop the stupid grin from spreading across his face.

The door sucked closed behind him, stirring the ghosts of cigar smoke and dust that lingered within. Will tipped his head back to take in the enormity of the space and let out a low whistle. This was the sort of place you could get lost in if you didn't leave a trail of breadcrumbs behind. He darted a glance in search of the woman from the alley— she didn't have much of a head start on him— but she was lost to the labyrinth of metal shelving that stretched through the warehouse as far as he could see.

For a moment he thought he heard the faint clicking of her heels. When Will turned toward the sound, a swell of soft jazz floated into the air.

He cast a glance back at the exit, a distinctly discomfiting feeling washing over him. But it was unsettling the way talking to a pretty girl was unsettling. Will's gaze roamed the shelves piled high with old roulette wheels, neon signs, and other remnants of forgotten dreams and he imagined an invisible line drawn before him on the dusty floor. Step over it and he would be irrevocably altered. Last chance to back out and stop whatever he'd set in motion here. The part of him that had kept himself locked into a stable job, no matter how mind-numbing, the part that didn't mind a hand-me-down couch and ramen noodles twice a week chided that he'd already had enough adventure here, what with the fountains and all. But the part of him that was fed up with the soul-suck that was his mortal existence had already decided he was all in, whatever the cost.

He crossed the line and set out in the direction of the sound, straining to hear more, but the only the scuff of his shoes on concrete echoed through the place. Will shook his head and wondered if he'd dreamt the music.

Each shelf he passed was laden with pieces of Las Vegas history— a marquee proclaiming *Live Tonight: DEAN MARTIN. Maybe Frank. Maybe Sammy,* boxes of film reels, martini glasses, event posters from the 1960s, neon signs from casinos long since imploded. He stepped closer and ran a finger over the aged felt of a blackjack table from a bygone era. Next his fingers found a collection of ancient poker chips, hundreds maybe thousands of them. He picked up a green-edged chip from the Sands and examined it in the light. He'd just started to roll it over his knuckles when he heard rustling from a nearby shelf.

"Hello," he called. His voice seemed to be swallowed by the immensity of the space.

A held breath. A heartbeat, two, then three.

"Can I help you?" a woman's voice called out, low and seductive. Something about it held the promise of nectar. It conjured up images of silken sheets and countless hours of pleasure. Was this the woman he'd seen? Something about the voice beckoned to the deeper parts of him, the same way that the lights of the city called to him, the flash of cards at the tables, the nightclubs draped with glittering women hungry for something to happen to them that would have to stay in Vegas.

Yes, he wanted to say. *Yes.* Filled with new purpose, he lit out in the direction of the voice. He hadn't had much wine from the fountain, but still he felt the beginnings of invincibility taking hold.

Help me. Happen to me. Unmake me and make me, a voice inside him called out.

Will peeked his head around the corner and his mind struggled to reconcile the face before him with the honeyed voice.

"Um, hello."

He fumbled for something more to say. He was at once repulsed and enthralled by the woman standing before him. She turned and in a trick of the light, Will could almost see the feathered headdress of a showgirl adorning her head. She'd been beautiful once, though long ago. It was there in her eyes and the set of her mouth, but the years had laid waste to the olive-skinned beauty. Limp grey curls framed her face where the skin hung like tissue paper over the fine bones of her face.

"Hello," she said. She didn't seem surprised to find him here. In fact, Will had the feeling that she'd known he was coming.

"The concierge at my hotel sent me. The door was unlocked so I just ..." Will said when he finally recovered the power of speech. "He told me I could find what I was looking for here."

"I suspect you will," said the faded beauty.

She inclined her head toward a set of doors at the opposite end of the warehouse and set off, her gossamer robe billowing behind her.

Will trotted to keep up— she was surprisingly lithe for her age— and at last ducked through the doors. Behind a set of beaded curtains the warehouse gave way to a place that was all candlelight and velvet and jazz. Couples swayed to the plaintive wail of trumpets. Groups of friends huddled in conversation at cocktail tables in the packed room. Maybe Will should have rummaged through the boxes in the warehouse for a tuxedo and bow tie to fit in with this crowd.

"What is this place?" he asked.

"A place for dreamers."

Before he could ask her to elaborate, the woman with the honeyed voice had left him at the edge of the room and melted into the crowd.

He scanned the room until his gaze landed on the young woman from the alley. She curled her ruby lips into a smile and assessed him in a way that made him think impure thoughts. Will looked over his shoulder, unsure he was the object of that heated look. But maybe this was his lucky night after all.

She crooked a slender finger to beckon him closer. Will hesitated, but only a moment before weaving through tables to close the distance between them. That smile again— it was starting. She held out a hand for his. He reached for her, but frowned when he made contact. Instead of the soft caress of fingers, cold plastic touched his palm. Will turned his hand over and examined the sleek card she'd offered and flipped it over. On one side was a magnetic strip and on the other, impossibly, his name.

"Hello, Mr. Davis. We've been expecting you."

***

Thirty minutes later a young man in an expensive suit jogged out to James's cab and handed him a crisp $100 bill.

89

"Thanks again, Mr. Gunning," the man said. He tapped the top of the cab before turning back in the direction of the emporium.

"Always a pleasure, Dino. See you next time."

He started the engine and went on his way.

***

On Monday, Will's supervisor, a disgruntled former child pageant star named Susie, was only mildly annoyed at another no call, no show. It wasn't until two weeks later when his landlord filed a missing persons report and the local news began to take interest that Susie, hair teased and skin freshly bronzed, made appearances. She dabbed at her eyes as she told a tragic story of an unknowable young man, not unlike James Dean, she said, in our lives for far too short a time.

Three months later, James Gunning tossed his keys on the counter after a long night of work and kissed his wife, Ida.

"Have you seen this story on the front page here?" Ida held up the morning paper.

"Which one is that?" James asked, but he didn't need to.

"The one about the guy who had the elephant in his hotel room. They say he died with millions of dollars lying on the floor all around him. The rich fool had a full recreation of the Sands casino floor in his suite. The original slot machines and poker chips and carpet and everything."

90

"Is that right?" James shook his head and unconsciously traced the outline of the poker chip in his pocket. He'd tuck it away in his sock drawer later. "Must be mighty hard to get an elephant in a hotel room."

"Right?" Ida threw her hands up. "Listen to this: 'The iconic Las Vegas sign— reported missing by a Minnesotan tourist group around eight o'clock last night— was found in one of the suite's bedrooms along with the fully grown elephant. The hotel's director of operations reports that they have no elevators large enough to accommodate an adult elephant, which can weigh anywhere from 4,000 to 7,000 pounds.How the animal got into Davis' hotel room remains a mystery. How Davis and his accomplices were able to steal the Las Vegas sign in broad daylight is still puzzling authorities as well. Metro hoped to find the culprits on tapes from the sign's security camera, but all surveillance footage had been replaced with duplicate coverage of the previous day.'"

James knew that little trick from way too many years of watching CSI.

"How'd they find him?" This part he didn't know.

"Floating in a bathtub filled with champagne," she said, delighted with a this new scandal. "He was wearing Frank Sinatra's tuxedo that he ripped off from the history museum."

Ripped off wasn't quite accurate, but James just raised his eyebrows and gave Ida his best surprised look.

"'An enigmatic man, gone way too soon,'" Ida finished in her newscaster voice. "Sad."

91

Sad, James thought, though it was the ghost of a smile, not a frown that graced his lips then. Gone too soon. At least, so they said.

But people died in hotel rooms more often than James's fares stiffed him for a tip. Ladies told their neighbors, who brought the news as new fodder for water cooler conversation. Memorials went up and construction workers traded the tales in the steel structures of their latest projects. Most of these stories caused a sensation then fizzled out in a week or so when people moved on, shocked and scandalized by something new. However, Will's demise and the peculiar circumstances of his last night made Will an enduring object of a national fascination. James kept a watchful eye out for any new news about Will as journalists and armchair detectives alike dug for new stories, new clues to the Will Davis enigma.

In the months that followed acquaintances came forward with stories of over the top Gatsby-esque parties thrown in Will's suite. Rumors —though unsubstantiated— floated around of a connection to a sheik in the Middle East. The hotel removed a piece of the outer wall of the penthouse suite and cameras rolled as a helicopter airlifted the elephant to solid ground. Volunteers combed surveillance tapes from every casino in Las Vegas casino but found no evidence of a big windfall for Davis. Barbara Walters interviewed Will's parents who assured her that there were certainly no rich relative to leave him thousands, let alone millions. As strange

92

evidence mounted, speculation on how a call center employee had managed to acquire a credit card with unlimited funds took over whole message boards. Theories flew back and forth on social media. TMZ even ran a special speculating whether he was the love child of the love child of Marilyn Monroe and JFK. Was he a drug mule? Was there a mob connection? And the elephant, how the hell did the elephant get in there?

***

Some year later James Gunning watched as the former mayor— martini in one hand and scissors in the other— cut the ribbon and people flooded into the new *Who Was Will Davis?* exhibit at the Las Vegas History museum. An unassuming man rolled a single match over his knuckles and wandered into the crowd.

The man sauntered up to the a life-size picture of Will taken in his hotel room the night before the body was found. He smiled at the image.

An aging docent appeared at his side. "Say, you look a lot like this Will Davis character."

The man chuckled, but angled his face away. "You think so?"

"You know, some people say he wasn't dead when they found him, that he's still out there somewhere."

"Hmmm." The hmmm was as neutral and pleasant as anyone could hope for. "I guess you never know."

*****

Winter Crossroads

By Richard J. Warren

The Saab crawled slowly south along Highway 93 through the small town of McGill. The gray skies were a gloomy sign of winter's imminent arrival. Every other storefront was vacant, yet there were plenty of people about. The old movie theater was boarded up but the hairstylist across the street was full of customers. Was the hamlet on its last legs or in the early stages of a rebound? Coop couldn't tell nor did he care, he just knew there was no Blackberry service here. He was relieved to reach the edge of town and be back at highway speed a few minutes later.

Several miles down the road he glanced in his rearview mirror and noticed a car rapidly approaching. He was contemplating pulling over to let the maniac pass when he saw the red and blue flashing lights come on as the cruiser neared his bumper. Heart racing, he quickly eyed the speedometer – two miles over the speed limit. *Was this guy for real?* He flipped on his turn signal and carefully moved to the right.

The cop pulled in behind him and got out of his vehicle, lights still flashing. Glancing in his side mirror, he saw the green-uniformed officer cautiously approach, right hand on the butt of his gun.

"License and registration please."

Coop reached slowly into the glove compartment hoping the cop wasn't trigger happy. He could imagine the headline: *Thirty-three-year-old William Cooper killed in rural Nevada by mistake.* It would cap off a perfect week. He retrieved the registration and handed it, along with his license, to the burly policeman with the shoulder patch of the White Pine County Sheriff.

"Did I do something wrong officer?" Coop asked. "I know I wasn't speeding."

"You were doing sixty-two in a sixty, but that's not why I pulled you over, Mr. Cooper. License says you're from Idaho. Where are you heading?"

"Phoenix, with a stop in Las Vegas."

"You'll never make it," the cop said. "You have something leaking from your vehicle."

Coop glanced at the instrument cluster and saw the water temperature was approaching the red zone. It was only then that he noticed a wisp of steam rising from under the hood. The officer gave him directions to a service station in the next town. He carefully pulled back onto the road with his eyes alternating between the temperature gauge, highway, and speedometer; the cop was following to make sure he made it.

Ten minutes later, temperature gauge now fully in the red and steam pouring out from the hood, he pulled into Cecil's Automotive in downtown Ely. Coop gave a wave of thanks to the cop as he pulled away and went to locate a mechanic, or whatever reasonable facsimile he could find in this godforsaken place. He could only imagine how much he was going to be ripped off for this repair, not that he'd know if he was being cheated or not. The sum total of his automotive knowledge could be distilled down to six words – oil in front, gas in back.

As he entered the dingy office his nostrils were assaulted by a mix of grease, motor oil, and stale cigars. Faded posters of bikini-clad girls holding various auto parts adorned the walls. The building appeared to be more than fifty years old and still sporting the original gunmetal gray paint job. The old wooden desk was covered with stains, littered with invoices, newspapers, magazines, and a parts manual dated 1997. At least the calendar was current and turned to the proper month, November, with one date circled in red – tomorrow, the 8th.

The door to the shop area opened and a man in a mechanic's uniform with the name "Muff" stitched on it entered. His gray and black hair was receding and tied back in a ponytail, and his moustache was all gray with a matching chin strip. He was heavily muscled and he must have been somewhere north of sixty, but Coop still wouldn't want to encounter him in a dark alley. After brief introductions, he followed him out to his still steaming car and noticed that the mechanic walked with a little bit of a limp.

As Muff popped the hood, Coop watched and tried to pretend that he knew what he was looking at. Truth is that this guy could tell him that "the rototemburtalator isn't construviating with the framus, thus causing a friction," and he'd just nod like the bobble-headed automotive ignoramus he was.

Muff played with a few things under the hood. "Here's your problem, upper heater hose has a hole in it. You wouldn't have gone much further."

"How long will it take to fix?" Coop asked.

"Take about twenty minutes – if I had the right hose. Not much need for yuppie-mobile parts here. I'll call around."

Coop stayed outside while the mechanic retreated to his office. The cold November air was better than the stench inside. He checked his Blackberry – still no service – he dreaded the thought of being here any longer than absolutely necessary. If someone had told him a few years ago that today he'd be stuck in a northern Nevada crossroads town shivering in the cold he would have surely thought they'd lost their mind. *How did he let this happen?*

It was all Angie's fault. He'd had it made, a rising star on Wall Street, barely thirty, with no limit to how far he could go. Perfect – or so he thought. Angie said she was homesick and wanted to move back to Boise to be near her family. He should have left her then, but no – he was too much of a wimp. Whatever Angie wanted, Angie got. Now it seemed she wanted everything but him.

He looked through the shop window and saw Muff talking on the phone and waving for him to come in. He reluctantly went through the door, bracing himself for the odor. The mechanic wrote something on a pad and hung up the phone.

"Good news, bad news, good news," Muff said. "I found the part, but it needs to be sent by FedEx. The good thing is it's still early enough to make today's pickup. It'll be here early afternoon tomorrow."

"Is there a decent hotel around here?"

"Hotel Nevada, about a mile up the road," Muff said. "You can't miss it; it used to be the tallest building in the state. I can give you a ride."

"Thanks, but I'll walk."

He strolled down the street holding his small gym bag feeling like he had stepped back into the 1950s. This town felt *old*. At another time he might have appreciated the quaintness of the locale and the mom-and-pop shops dotting the main drag. Today he just wanted to get as far away from here, from Boise, and Angie, as possible. He began to walk down the street as the sun was fading away. He zipped up his jacket as the cold wind whipped through him and chilled him to the bone.

He found the hotel easy enough; he hoped the building-sized mural of a cowboy-attired pig cooking bacon and eggs in a frying pan wasn't an omen. He counted the floors – six– and marveled at the fact that this had once been

Nevada's tallest structure. Something else he found odd was the dozen or so motorcycles parked out front. This wasn't exactly bike-riding season. He looked toward the sky just as a few flakes of snow began to fall.

He went inside and his lungs were instantly filled with secondhand smoke just as his ears were assaulted by the piped in country music. He found the registration desk. It was also the bell desk, the casino cashier, the switchboard, first-aid station, the lost and found, and probably everything else imaginable. He handed his credit card and driver's license to the clerk and his eyes wandered as she prepared the paperwork. The interior of the hotel looked like a hunting lodge. There were stuffed animals and birds everywhere including mountain lions, wolves, moose, deer, beaver, hawks, owls, with some rattlesnakes thrown in for good measure. The hotel certainly didn't have the PETA seal of approval though Wild Kingdom probably gave it four stars.

After he checked in he took the key and went up to his floor. The lone elevator creaked and groaned as it struggled to make its way to the fifth level. He eyed the photo of a local copper mine with the caption imploring him to extend his stay and take in the sights; *if that's the main tourist attraction, God help me.* He found his room and read the plaque on the door that said this was the "Jimmy Stewart Suite." Apparently many of the rooms were named after some famous person who had the misfortune of having stayed there at one time. Inside everything looked old except for the flat-screen TV, strangely out of place mounted on the wall across from the bed. The room was small but it had a bed, right now he just wanted a nap.

Later that evening he went down to the coffee shop. Worn-out red vinyl booths and chipped tabletops highlighted the décor; the place was in major need of a makeover to say the least. Pictures of NASCAR drivers adorned the walls. There must have been a rule requiring the waitresses to be a minimum of fifty pounds overweight, smell like stale cigarettes, and be missing at least one tooth. He was trapped in redneck hell.

After dinner he went for a walk, but the temperature had dropped precipitously with the setting sun, so he didn't go far. He walked past the few motorcycles remaining out front and shook his head. How could anyone ride in this cold? He checked his Blackberry and saw he had a weak signal so he hit the button for voicemail but the call dropped before he could connect. He looked at the display again; the signal was gone. He stopped in front of a Harley and shivered as he drew his jacket tighter and shook his head at the thought of being on a motorcycle in this weather and muttered, "Morons."

"You say something?" asked someone behind him.

He turned around and found himself facing a gray-haired mountain of a man that must have outweighed him by a hundred pounds. The perfect caricature of a Hell's Angel, along with a scowl, he was wearing blue jeans and a leather vest with a bandana tied around his head. His bare arms were heavily tattooed and even more heavily muscled. Coop needed to learn to keep his big mouth shut.

"I didn't say anything," he said.

"I think you did prissy-boy."

Two more bikers came over and were now in a circle around him. He was looking for a way out. The hotel door was no more than ten feet away but there was eight-hundred pounds of big, bad, biker dudes between him and it.

"Look," he pleaded, "I don't want any trouble."

"No trouble at all, shit-for-brains," the second biker said. "We'd be happy to kick your ass."

"Leave him alone dickheads," boomed a voice from behind him.

It was Muff. The posture of the bikers changed instantly and they backed away. Muff came forward and Coop saw he was dressed in full biker attire. Certainly not someone Coop would normally associate with, right now he was a sight for sore eyes.

"C'mon," Muff said. "I'll buy you a drink."

The hotel bar ran the length of one wall. It was a typical setup with a mirrored backsplash and bottles arranged on shelves above and below the counter. He thought it funny that the phone had something you don't see any more– a cord! There was an old Elvis clock on the wall that was very likely installed when the singer was still alive. The most interesting feature may have been the bartender. It was barely thirty degrees outside and he was wearing shorts. He sported a mullet hairstyle that he likely wore in high school twenty-five years ago. The bartender walked over toward the two of them.

"Hey Muff; Jack and Coke?"

"Yeah Willie," Muff replied. "Get my friend here whatever he's having."

Coop asked for a bottled beer figuring it was safe and watched as Willie poured Muff a Coke without the booze. He set the drinks down in front of them and walked away without asking for money.

"He forgot your Jack Daniels," Coop said.

"Nah, he didn't, he just asks to make me feel good. Doctor told me my liver is toast and I can't drink that shit anymore. I allow myself one shot a year. That quack also told me I was going to be dead in six months – that was ten years ago. What'd you say your name was?"

"William Cooper, everybody calls me Coop."

"So, Coop, what brings you to Ely?"

"Passing through on my way to Phoenix; heading for a new job and better weather."

"What about your family?"

"Don't have any, not any more. My wife left me."

"What'd you do?"

"Why does everyone think it's me? I didn't do anything! You don't even know me. I gave that bitch everything she wanted, but it wasn't enough."

"I sense just a wee bit of hostility," Muff said. "Let me guess – she left you for another man."

"Her high school sweetheart; they reconnected through Facebook. She begs me to move back to Boise because she's homesick. Two years later I find out the real reason; I come home from work and she tells me she's moving in with that prick. Of course by then I'd thrown everything away."

"So you're feeling somewhat emasculated?"

The surprise showed on Coop's face. "Interesting choice of words for a biker-slash-mechanic."

"Believe it or not, I used to be an accountant. I got out of the Army and wanted to make something of my life. Put myself through school on the GI Bill so I could be a slick bean counter, but I was an angry young man – just like you. Then one day a head-on collision almost killed me. After I recovered, I started thinking about what was really important; it wasn't a suit and tie or the yuppie crap. It was time for me to stop doing what everyone said I was supposed to and just be my true self. I told my wife I was ditching the bullshit and gave her the option to come along. She told me to have a nice life but not before cleaning me out. A bunch of twist and turns brought me here and I never left."

"And now you work at Cecil's garage," Coop said.

"I own Cecil's – I'm Cecil Langdon. Muff's a nickname my ex-wife stuck on me."

"You're my hero," Coop said. "You got out of the rat race."

"Bullshit. All you have to do is stop running away."

"I'm not running from anything."

"Yes you are," Muff said. "You're running from your ex-wife and the expectations this screwed up society placed on you; mostly you're running from yourself."

With that Muff got up and left. Willie came over and cleared the glasses and wiped the counter. As Muff's words echoed in his head, the bells of the slot machines rang in the background, a Nashville singer was wailing about being angry all the time, and some customer was hacking up a lung in a phlegm-filled spasm.

"How long you in town for?" Willie asked.

"I'm out of here tomorrow as soon as my car's fixed."

"You should stick around. Tomorrow's the 8th, a big day for Muff."

"I Can't."

Coop's car wasn't finished until late afternoon the next day. He threw his bag in the trunk and went inside the office to settle up. Whatever it cost would be worth it after Muff came to his rescue the night before. Muff handed him the keys.

"How much do I owe you?"

"There's no charge," Muff said.

"Don't be ridiculous. How much is it?"

105

"I'm serious," Muff said. "All repairs are free on November 8th, always have been."

"Then why isn't this place packed?"

"I guess people don't want to take advantage."

He looked at the calendar on the wall and again saw the red circle around today's date.

"But why? What's the big deal about today? Is it your birthday or something?"

"Or something," Muff said. "Come down to the hotel at eight tonight."

"I can't."

Coop left and started driving out of town. He glanced at his watch, almost six. Why did he feel as if was doing something wrong by leaving? He didn't fit in with these people and he needed to be on his way. But he'd been stuck here for more than a day already, what difference would a few more hours make? Besides, he was at least a little curious. He turned around and made his way back.

Coop walked into the hotel twenty minutes before eight. Every stool was strangely empty even though there were a lot of people near the bar. He made a move to sit down when his arm was grabbed by one of the bikers who had accosted him the night before.

"Don't even think about it, prissy-boy."

He backed off and noticed that all the bikers were there but respectfully staying a few feet back from the bar.

Several hotel guests were milling around looking to see what the fuss was all about. Willie carefully wiped down the counter and started putting down shot glasses – dozens of shot glasses – he counted forty-eight in all. When they were lined up down the length of the bar, Willie pulled out a couple of bottles of Jack Daniels. He glanced at the clock – seven forty-five – and started to pour the booze, finishing his task just before the top of the hour.

At precisely eight several heads turned toward the entrance and Coop's gaze followed along. Muff walked in wearing an old, green Army uniform. There was a shoulder patch with an angel's wing holding a sword that said Airborne, sergeant stripes on the sleeves, his chest festooned with medals and ribbons. Coop didn't know what most of them were, but he did recognize a Purple Heart, Bronze Star, Combat Infantry Badge, and Paratrooper Wings. Muff's cap, which appeared new, was a maroon beret sporting an insignia that said 173rd Airborne.

The hotel was eerily quiet. Even the slot machines had gone silent; he saw that they'd actually been turned off. He looked at the other bikers and noticed, while not in uniform, many of them had military insignias and medals of their own. Muff walked solemnly to the center of the bar and stood rigidly at attention. The bikers did their best to follow suit and even Coop found himself standing a bit straighter.

In unison they bowed their heads in a moment of silence. Muff then took two steps forward and hoisted a shot glass.

"To my fallen brothers." He downed the shot in one gulp.

When Muff placed the glass down the others stepped forward. Willie motioned toward Coop that he should join in. He stepped up and drank a shot. They drank until they were all gone. Coop looked over at Muff and saw the tears streaming down his face. With military precision that would make any drill sergeant proud, Muff turned ninety degrees and marched out the door.

Willie cleaned up the bar and everyone dispersed with hardly a word. Coop waited until he could catch Willie's attention.

"What the hell was that all about?"

Willie looked at Coop and his expression softened. "Muff was a platoon sergeant in Vietnam. His company was overrun by twelve-hundred Viet Cong; they were outnumbered twenty to one and didn't have a chance. Forty-eight of his guys were killed, the handful that weren't were wounded, including him; that's why he walks with a limp. That was November 8th, 1965."

Later that night Coop was headed south on his way to Las Vegas, unable to organize his thoughts in any way that fit the world as he thought he knew it. About an hour outside of Ely he pulled into a rest area. Events of the past day and a half left him feeling confused. He wasn't sure where his life would lead from here but he knew the answers weren't waiting in Phoenix. He got out of his car and opened the trunk, pulled out his garment bag with all his suits and tossed it in a dumpster.

He pulled his car back toward the road and glanced at the sign indicating Las Vegas is 175 miles to the south – he turned north toward Ely. Just as he got up to highway speed he grabbed his Blackberry and tossed it out the open window.

*****

Memories of Jay MacLarty

Jay MacLarty

1943 – 2010

Jay MacLarty was born in Spirit Lake, Iowa, and grew up in the Midwest (Iowa, Nebraska, and Minnesota). As an adult, he had lived for extended periods in Florida, California, Nevada, and Colorado. He was a successful restaurateur, horse-racing handicapper, software developer and always an avid reader. Jay finally turned his attention toward the written word, working nights and weekends on a lengthy and sweeping ethnic saga. The manuscript was "well reviewed," but judged "too long and literary" for a first-time novelist, and he was told to "go write the popular book first."

That book became *The Courier* – the first in a series starring common-man hero Simon Leonidovich – a high-tech thriller, drawing on Jay's unique background of business, politics, and high technology. That novel was followed by *Bagman*, *Live Wire*, and *Choke Point*. All four books have received literary recognition.

The Las Vegas writers' community is grateful for Jay's role in founding and guiding the Las Vegas Writers' Group. LVWG brings together novice and established essayists, poets, novelists and journalists to share experiences and ideas. As a mentor, Jay will always be remembered fondly. Vibrant and warm, he inspired with his energy, intellect and wit.

Writers often lament the fact that writing is a solitary pursuit. But I've come to believe—something Jay knew all those years ago when he started the Las Vegas Writers Group—that it doesn't have to be that way. Writing is a collaborative process. We need others who get us: people we can trust to bounce ideas off of, to catch the things we miss, and to hug us and give us wine as we alternate between delusions of grandeur and soul-crushing doubt. It was in this group that I found those people for the first time. Here I met the people who would become my critique partners and life-long friends, and found the courage to share my work for the first time. For that I will be forever grateful to Jay McLarty – the man who started it all.

– Jessica Cline

My grandmother had this theory about life. She believed that life as we know it is Purgatory, the mythical place where souls are sent to atone for previous sins before entering Heaven. As I get older, and life takes from me people I hold dear, I'm beginning to ascribe to her theory. As I'm writing this, the holidays are upon us, and at no other time during the year do I feel the absence of friends and loved ones more fully and profoundly.

Jay was a man lit from within by the joy of writing and storytelling. Like moths to flame, those harboring the flicker of hope to tell their own stories felt Jay's inimitable pull. And Jay welcomed, encouraged, supported, and chastised each, pushing them up the ladder, climbing toward realization of their dreams.

As Holly, Jay's wife, told me, Jay would've hated all this fuss made in his memory, but, well, too bad, Jay. This is a way to keep the light he lit burning. A way to keep building his fledgling group of writers, so that more of us have the thrill of seeing our words brought to light.

This was Jay's dream. He is missed every day by those of us who knew him well. This project helps to bring him closer, and keep his dreams alive. I like that.

– Deborah Coonts

I always liked Jay MacLarty because of his constant intensity in trying to help other writers. He was passionate about getting information, as he saw it, as he knew it, to help newer writers become professional, published authors, as he was. Jay used to say writing his novels came hard for him. Five hundred words a day were all he could manage, yet, when he was done with his daily work, he would say "but my pages are pristine." Jay and I disagreed on many things about writing and what helps other writers, but how could I not respect someone working hard at what is hard for him, then sharing his hard-won lessons to make it easier for others?

Jay was not only one of the founding fathers of the Las Vegas Writers Group but he was always the engine and the spirit of our group. His influence remains. Jay spearheaded the concept of the critique group, championing it, seeking feedback from others for his own successful body of work. Jay deeply believed in "writer teamwork," writers being supportive of each other, and Jay gave credit to others when he got help. He showed me, openly, his own way of plotting novels, a large elaborate scene outline, taped on the wall above his computer, a big, busy chart, color-coded, with boxes and arrows; he shared what he had learned, always.

116

He applied the same intelligence and discipline that he applied to other career efforts throughout his life. He found time to champion writers, and offer any help he could give to other writers, often through and for The Las Vegas Writers Group, where he modestly never took a title. I very recently was awarded the *Jay MacLarty Founder's Award* for 2013 and frankly questioned if I deserved it, until it was pointed out to me that this was for the spirit of what Jay MacLarty brought to our group, year after year; framed in that way, carrying on for Jay, I now feel very good about it.

Jay, wherever you're now organizing critique groups, I will always consider your generous-of-spirit work in this area of helping others something that, yes, Jay, was definitely pristine.

– John Hill

I never had the pleasure of getting to know Jay McLarty personally, but I, like many others have flourished as a writer because of his passion for the craft. Jay has been a source of inspiration to authors through his leadership and educational endeavors. He has created a safe place for writers to learn, commiserate and support each other through this beautiful minefield of the written word. His spirit lives on in the work of everyone he has inspired and I am forever grateful.

– Sheryl Greenblatt

Jay MacLarty was a great friend and mentor to many writers in Las Vegas. I am honored to have known him. He had a great, wry sense of humor and really cared about fostering a vibrant, thriving writing community here in the neon desert that is Las Vegas. Sometimes it's hard to believe that he's really gone. But I hope his memory will live on and inspire a new batch of young writers to look at their work with a critical eye and tell the best, most well-crafted, fully imagined stories they can.

– Eric James Miller

I was an author of a non-fiction book on real estate investing and wrote a column for a national real estate publication. My actual interest was in writing fiction. With this in mind I searched for events related to writing and stumbled across a website for the Las Vegas Writers Group. It looked promising so I thought I would attend the next meeting and see what it was all about.

I walked into the meeting room and was immediately greeted by a friendly, non-assuming gentleman who not only introduced himself, but invited me over to his table and offered me a slice of his pizza. He asked what I was working on. I told him I was looking to transition from non-fiction to fiction and shared my idea for a novel. His eyes lit up and the conversation quickly became a lively one as he shared his thoughts on plotting and character development. Who is this guy, I wondered?

That man was Jay MacLarty. I soon found out that he was not only a writer, but a very successful one. His passion for the written word and a genuine willingness to share his knowledge and help fellow writers told me I had found a home with the group. After my third monthly meeting Jay and Vic

120

asked if I would be willing to help out as a volunteer. I didn't hesitate for a minute.

When Vic needed to step down as Organizer Jay asked if I would be willing to run the group. He knew I had a business background with experience running seminars and other types of meetings and would be able to handle the group. Jay's preference was to remain in the background, a place where he felt better able to help others. I saw it as an opportunity to give back to the writing community in the same way Jay had. Little did I know that we would lose him a little more than a year later. I consider it both an obligation and an honor to carry on Jay's legacy.

– Richard J. Warren

I met Jay when I attended a meeting of the Las Vegas Writers Group for the first time in 2008. He smiled and greeted each new member. His welcoming presence made me feel comfortable enough to keep going to meetings. As years passed, I came to know Jay not only as a supportive and encouraging asset to the group, but a humble writer who I never heard brag about his publishing credits. He sat and talked to people about their writing. He gave advice freely and directly--none of the beating around the proverbial bush for Jay! Sometimes he'd shout out a comment during meetings, adding his wisdom and experience to the conversation, and almost always generating a chuckle. Even amongst fellow writers he had a way with words, and his wonderful sense of humor is just one more reason he is sorely missed.

– Lindsay Wright

Meet the Authors

Jessica Cline

Jessica Cline is a longtime member of the Las Vegas Writers Group and writer of fantastical stories. She's stomped grapes in her native California, hiked 350 miles on an ancient pilgrimage route in Spain, had breakfast with a coatimundi in Costa Rica, and spent the night in a monastery. But no matter where life takes her, her favorite place is still curled up on the couch watching *Doctor Who* with her husband and two boys.

Deborah Coonts

My mother tells me I was born a very long time ago, but I'm not so sure—my mother can't be trusted. These things I do know: I was raised in Texas on barbeque, Mexican food and beer. I currently reside in Las Vegas, where my friends assure me I cannot get into too much trouble. Silly people. I am the author of WANNA GET LUCKY? (A NY Times Notable Crime Novel for 2010 and double RITA™ Finalist), LUCKY STIFF, SO DAMN LUCKY and four digital novellas, LUCKY IN LOVE, LUCKY BANG and LUCKY NOW AND THEN, Parts One and Two. The fourth Lucky novel, LUCKY BASTARD was just released May 14th in hardcover. I can usually be found at the bar, but also at www.deborahcoonts.com.

Sheryl Greenblatt

Sheryl Greenblatt is a Long Island, NY native who has been living (and thawing) in Las Vegas for approximately five years now. She writes mystery novels, works as a freelance writer and is the proud mother of an eight year old Beagle/ Yellow Lab rescue named after Anne Rice's Mother of all Vampires. Thankfully, the dog has not yet developed a taste for human blood. Sheryl is currently the President of the *Writers of Southern Nevada* and contributes articles to Examiner.com covering the topic of *Pets in Las Vegas*.

Sheryl was the winner of the 2012 *Jay MacLarty Founder's Award.*

John Hill

John Hill was a full-time professional Hollywood TV and screenwriter from 1974- 1999. His credits include *Griffin and Phoenix* (1976), *Heartbeeps* (1981), co-writer of *Little Nikita* (1988) and *Quigley Down Under,* (1990). He has worked on staff as a writer-type producer on *Quantum Leap* and on *L.A. Law*, where he won an Emmy in 1991. He now teaches writing and filmmaking at the University of Nevada in Las Vegas, where he lives with his wife Nancy.

John was the winner of the 2013 *Jay MacLarty Founders Award.*

Holly McKinnis

Holly McKinnis grew up in Las Vegas and is constantly surprised by the speed it grows and changes. At night, she dresses nudes in a production show on the strip. In the day, she pounds the keyboard while plotting crimes and disasters.

Holly has been a member of the LVWG since its inception in 2004.

Eric James Miller

Eric James Miller is an author and part-time paranormal investigator who lives in Las Vegas, Nevada. *For Rent: Dangerous Paradise*, the first novel in his For Rent Mystery Series was published in August 2013. It was inspired, in part, by an actual missing person case and an odd little apartment building in Venice Beach, California where he lived for several years. The second novel in the series *For Rent: Haunted Neon* is due to be released in early 2014. It follows spunky young journalist Dana Santoyo from Venice to Las Vegas, where she will move into the motel described at the end of his short story "The Ghost of John Bartlett."

Richard J. Warren

Following a career as a Certified Financial Planner, Richard J. Warren moved to Las Vegas from Long Island, New York in 2003. He is an author and freelance journalist and currently the Consumer Columnist for *The Vegas Voice*. A seasoned real estate investor, he is the author of *A Rehabber's Tale, The Reality of Fixing and Flipping Real Estate* and has written more than 150 articles related to real estate investing.

Richard is the Organizer and Director of the Las Vegas Writers Group. In addition he serves on the Board of Directors of the *Writers of Southern Nevada*, a non-profit organization dedicated to providing education and resources to writers.

Lindsay Wright

Lindsay Wright began writing stories at the age of seven when her grandma gave her a blank journal as a gift. Most of those stories were about animals or mean things her brothers did to her. Today she always has multiple works in progress. She runs, sews, dances badly, and is the Program Director for the Las Vegas Writers Group. Writing remains her number #2 love--her cat is #1, of course.

Lindsay was the winner of the *2011 Jay MacLarty Founder's Award.*

132

www.ingramcontent.com/pod-product-compliance
Lightning Source LLC
Chambersburg PA
CBHW071310130626
46556CB00004B/1549